Dan brushed a tangle of hair away from his daughter's face, then gave her a gentle kiss on her forehead. "Love you, munchkin."

"Love you, punchkin," the little girl repeated with a giggle.

Dan smoothed her hair again, smiling at her, the love for his daughter softening his features.

Hailey swallowed as she watched the scene between father and daughter. She always knew Dan would make a good father.

Her heart twisted with old sorrow and old regrets and a flurry of "what ifs."

She pressed her eyes shut a moment, as if to close her mind to the past. One quick breath and the memories were gone. When she opened her eyes she caught Dan's frown.

She flashed him a quick smile as if to let him know that everything was just fine. Then she took Natasha's hand and led her to the table.

It was fine, she assured herself. Everything was, indeed, just fine.

But it was also just temporary.

Books by Carolyne Aarsen

Love Inspired

A Bride at Last
The Cowboy's Bride
†*A Family-Style Christmas*
†*A Mother at Heart*
†*A Family at Last*
A Hero for Kelsey
Twin Blessings
Toward Home
Love Is Patient
A Heart's Refuge
Brought Together by Baby
A Silence in the Heart
Any Man of Mine
Yuletide Homecoming
Finally a Family
A Family for Luke
The Matchmaking Pact
Close to Home
Cattleman's Courtship
Cowboy Daddy
The Baby Promise
*The Rancher's Return
The Cowboy's Lady
*Daddy Lessons

†Stealing Home
*Home to Hartley Creek

CAROLYNE AARSEN

and her husband, Richard, live on a small ranch in northern Alberta, where they have raised four children and numerous foster children, and are still raising cattle. Carolyne crafts her stories in an office with a large west-facing window through which she can watch the changing seasons while struggling to make her words obey.

Daddy Lessons

Carolyne Aarsen

Love Inspired

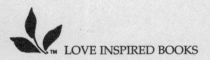 ™ LOVE INSPIRED BOOKS

ISBN-13: 978-0-373-87728-7

DADDY LESSONS

Copyright © 2012 by Carolyne Aarsen

This edition published by arrangement with Love Inspired Books.

www.LoveInspiredBooks.com

Printed in U.S.A.

Oh, the depths of the riches of the wisdom and knowledge of God! How unsearchable His judgments and His paths beyond tracing out.

—*Romans* 11:33

As a writer I am so thankful
that I don't work alone. I want to thank my editor,
Tina James, for her hard work and patient guidance
in shaping my stories.

Chapter One

"C'mon, honey, we've got to get going. You don't want to be late for your first day of school." Dan Morrow tossed his daughter's backpack over his shoulder and reached for Natasha to help her down from the truck.

Bright orange buses pulled up along the sidewalk of Hartley Creek Elementary School, spilling out their loads of children. Some ran, some walked and some trudged up the sidewalk, their winter coats wide open, ignoring the chilly wind swirling snow around the school yard.

British Columbia mountain weather, Dan thought with a shudder.

But Natasha sat on the truck seat, her hands folded over her stomach, her brown hair hiding her face and falling down the front of her bright red winter jacket.

"My tummy still hurts," she said, peeking through her hair, adding a wince in case he didn't believe her. "And I still miss my mommy." Natasha sniffed, her brown eyes shimmering with tears.

Despite her performance of variations on the same theme for the past few minutes, his heart still twisted at her words. Though he and Lydia had been divorced for five years, Dan was still dealing with his ex-wife's recent death.

He couldn't imagine what his little girl, who had lived with Lydia up until her death a month ago, was going through.

He pressed a kiss to Natasha's head. "I know you're sad, honey," he said, tucking her hair behind her ear so he could see her face. "But school is starting and you don't want to be late, do you?" He made his voice reasonable and soothing, hoping she would move.

The bell sounded and the last of the stragglers entered the school. Dan tossed a quick glance toward the grade one classroom directly ahead of him. Kids moved past the frosted windows, getting settled into their desks. A taller figure stopped, looking out the window. Even from here, he caught the red-gold shine of Hailey Deacon's hair, that little tilt of her head that told him she was watching them. He'd seen her stop before to look out the window and watch them as soon as they pulled into the parking lot.

He tried not to let his heart flip the way it always did whenever he saw her, back when they were dating.

Since he and Natasha had come back to Hartley Creek, he'd managed to avoid Hailey, his old girlfriend. But she worked as a teacher's aide in the grade one class his daughter was supposed to attend. A first meeting between them was inevitable.

Dan turned back to Natasha, his concern for his daughter taking priority.

"I don't want to go." Her raised voice echoed over the now-empty school yard. "I want to stay with you."

"I know, but you have to start school. And I need to get back to work at Grandpa's hardware store."

He was about to tug on Natasha's arm again when a glint of reflected light from the school's door caught his attention. The door fell closed and there she was, her coat open, her hair flowing like a copper flag behind her.

As she came closer he saw the concern on her delicate

features, the frown above her gray eyes. His heart flipped again.

Everything has changed, he reminded himself, turning back to Natasha. *You were married. You've got a daughter. You lost your chance with her. Stay out of the past.*

"We're going now," he said to his daughter, trying to sound as if he was in charge.

But Natasha just looked ahead, her arms clasped tightly over her stomach.

"Sorry to barge in," Hailey was saying. "But I noticed from the window you were having some trouble."

Dan steeled himself, then turned to face his old girlfriend. She brushed a strand of hair back from her face as a hesitant smile played around the edges of her mouth. She looked as beautiful as she ever had. Maybe even more so. Old emotions seeped up from where he thought they were buried. He pushed them down. He had no right to get distracted.

"Natasha is upset," he said curtly. "She doesn't want to go to school."

"Of course she's sad," Hailey replied, coming around to stand beside him. Then Hailey gave him a sympathetic look that almost found its way through the barriers he had thrown up. "I'm sorry to hear about your wife."

"Ex-wife."

She pulled back from him, his tone obviously accomplishing what he wanted—to keep her at arm's length and protect himself.

"I heard about that too." She attempted another smile, then turned back to Natasha.

Dan looked down at the top of Hailey's head. She still parted her hair in that jagged line, still let it hang free over her shoulders, still wore perfume that smelled like oranges.

He clenched his fists and turned his wavering attention back to his daughter.

"Hello, Natasha, my name is Miss Deacon." Hailey held her hand out. "I'll be helping you in school this morning."

She had pitched her voice to the same low, reassuring level she used when she taught children how to ski and snowboard on the ski hill.

"I don't want to go to school," Natasha said, turning to Dan, her voice breaking. Her cries tore at Dan's heart. He couldn't leave her like this. But neither could he take Natasha back to the apartment above the hardware store. His father was recuperating from an extreme case of bronchial pneumonia. His mother worked at his hardware store and couldn't watch Natasha. Dan didn't know anyone who could babysit during the day.

He cleared his throat, embarrassed that Hailey had to witness his lack of control over his daughter. "I'm sorry, Natasha, but it's time for school."

He tried to get his arms around her to lift her out of the truck, but she swung out at him. "I don't want to go. Don't make me go." Her feet flailed in their heavy winter boots, hitting him in the arm. She wasn't going willingly.

Now what should he do? Drag her into the building?

"Dan, can I talk to you?" Hailey asked, catching his arm.

He shot her a puzzled glance and Hailey immediately released him, rubbing her hand against her pants, as if wiping away his touch.

As they walked away from the truck, Natasha's cries grew louder and more demanding.

"If I can get her into the classroom, I'm sure she'll be okay," Dan insisted. "She just needs to know who's in charge. Her mother always let her do whatever she wanted."

Hailey sighed and he got the impression she didn't agree with him. Big surprise. Hailey had always been the kind of girl who went her own way, did her own thing.

And you're judging her after all the things you did?

The old guilt rose up again, a feeling that nagged at him as much as his self-reproach over his brother's death seven years ago.

"Natasha has had a lot to deal with in the last few weeks," Hailey was saying. "Things have happened to her she had no control over and now she's trying to find a way to take back some of that lost control. This is how she'll do it."

She sounded reasonable and, thankfully, practical. They were simply two adults discussing what to do about a little girl.

"But I need to get to work," he said, glancing back at Natasha. "My mother needs me at the store now that Dad isn't doing so well."

"I know that and you should go." Hailey put her hand on his arm again. He was sure her gesture was automatic, but even through the thickness of his jacket her touch still managed to hit him square in the gut.

This time he jerked away.

"How will that work?" he asked, shoving his hands in the pockets of his jacket.

"The store isn't that far from here." Hailey folded her arms over her chest. "I suggest you leave the truck here and walk to the store. I'll stay here with her until she's ready to come inside."

Dan frowned, glancing from Natasha back to Hailey. "Don't you need to get to the classroom?"

"Right now, my priority is your daughter. She won't sit in that truck all day and even if she does that's okay. To-morrow we might have to do it again, but eventually she'll get tired of sitting outside. If we let her make the decision, hopefully she'll feel as if she has some say in the matter. Once that happens, she can slowly move into a routine which will help her in the healing process."

"It seems like a lot of trouble," he said, glancing over at Natasha, who had quieted down and was watching them with interest. "What if it takes all day?"

"I'm not that busy in the classroom today. Two days of the week I only work half-time. Today is one of those days."

"So what do you do the other half of those days?"

As soon as he spoke he felt like hitting himself on the forehead. That was none of his business.

He was also surprised to see a faint flush color Hailey's cheeks. "I volunteer at the ski hill. Visit my Nana."

Her comment reminded him of her reason for her temporary return to Hartley Creek. "I heard about her heart attack. I'm sorry. I knew you and your sisters are very close to her. How is she feeling?"

Hailey tipped her head down, fingering a gold necklace hanging around her neck. "She's doing very well. Thanks for asking."

The little hitch in her voice kindled concern for her and resurrected memories and emotions he thought he'd dealt with long ago.

He blinked, mentally pushing them away. Natasha and her care was his priority right now. Hailey didn't even make the list. Besides, he had heard she was leaving town at the end of the school year.

He shifted his weight, trying to decide what to do, then glanced at his watch and his decision was made for him. Time was running out.

"Okay. I'll leave you with her," he said with a resigned sigh. "But if you need me, call me at the store." He reached in his shirt pocket for his pen and the pad of paper he always carried around.

She held up her hand in a stop gesture. "I know the number."

Of course she would remember. When they were dating, he worked at his father's store after school and she would call him every day.

He shook off the memory as he glanced past her to his daughter, who still watched them with an intent gaze as if trying to figure out what they were talking about.

"Just so you know, she's incredibly stubborn and strong-willed." His heart shifted at the sight of her, so small, sitting in the truck, her feet straight out. "But she really needs a routine in her life and the sooner the better." Then he turned back to Hailey. "You call me if she gets upset or needs me."

"I will," Hailey promised.

Still he hesitated. He'd had to walk away from Natasha so many times; he didn't want to do it again. At least this time he would see her in a few hours instead of a few weeks.

"I should say goodbye to her before I go," he said.

Natasha's expression grew hopeful when he approached the truck. He bent over and gave her a quick kiss and a hug. "I'm going to the store, honey. You can stay here in the truck, like you wanted."

Puzzlement creased her forehead as Dan straightened. She seemed unsure of this new twist in her plans.

He stepped away, fighting his own urge to give in to her. He zipped up his coat and walked toward Hailey. "You'll let me know how things go?"

"I'll make sure she's okay."

Dan gave her a tight nod, but before he left, their gazes met and held and it seemed as if the intervening years slipped away. Seven years of living away from Hartley Creek and a failed marriage drifted away like smoke with one look into those gray-blue eyes.

Then the past slid into the present and with it came reality.

He had Natasha, his greatest blessing and the only positive consequence of his marriage.

"Talk to you later," was his gruff response as he steeled himself against old emotions.

At one time he had loved Hailey. At one time they'd made plans. Then Austin's death had crashed into their lives and with it had come a flood of guilt. Dan had promised his parents, who didn't like for their sons to go snowboarding, that he would watch over Austin. He'd failed them when Austin died on a run he should never have started.

And then Hailey had broken up with him.

He straightened his shoulders. Hailey belonged to his past, not his present.

"Adam, come here," Hailey called out to the little boy who was about to run out of the school with no coat, no hat and no scarf. The temperature hovered around minus ten with the wind. The kid's ears would freeze and his mother, Emma Minton, would be annoyed.

Adam sighed, and turned around, trudging back to her, dragging his coat and his backpack. "Why do I have to put on my coat? It gets so hot in the bus."

Hailey knelt down. "If something happens, we want you to be properly dressed."

As she helped him with his coat, the doors at the end of the noisy hallway opened up again. A tall figure strode around the much smaller bodies, shifting to avoid the headlong rush of children released from the confines of the class.

Although she had seen Dan Morrow every afternoon for the past week, each time an echo of her old feelings lifted her heart.

He was taller than he had been in high school; his shoulders had filled out and broadened. His blond hair had darkened, his face had gained a few more lines, but it was his gaze that snagged and held her attention.

His deep-set eyes used to mesmerize and melt her heart. Now they looked at her with a calm indifference that hurt her more than anger would have.

You broke up with him because he wanted to leave. Why do you care how he looks at you?

The question mocked her as she forced her attention back to Adam, who was squirming like a snake.

Dan reached for the door to the class, but Hailey held out a hand to stop him. "Natasha's teacher, Miss Tolsma, wants to talk to you before you take Natasha home," she said.

"Why?"

Hailey hesitated, then angled him a quick glance. "Today was not…not Natasha's best day," she said, deliberately keeping her comment vague in front of Adam, Natasha's classmate.

"At least she got out of the truck right away today," Dan said, with a hopeful note in his voice. He shot a quick glance through the window in the classroom door at his daughter, who sat perched at the edge of a tiny chair, clutching her backpack.

Hailey followed his glance and suppressed a sigh as she zipped up Adam's coat.

It was Friday afternoon and school was done for the week. As he had the past four days, Dan had come to pick

Natasha up. Megan Tolsma had asked Hailey to tell Dan she needed to talk to him. However, Megan was still in a staff meeting, leaving Hailey to fill the awkward silence between her and Dan with idle chitchat.

At one time Hailey could have regaled Dan with stories about people they knew. Passed on a bit of gossip. Talked about the snow conditions on the mountain.

Now their history and the silence of the past seven years yawned like a chasm between them, and above that space floated memories of Austin's death. The tragic event that pushed them apart. That sent Dan west to Vancouver and Hailey in the opposite direction.

Dan drummed his fingers against his thigh, obviously also aware of the awkwardness trembling between them.

Hailey dragged her attention back to Adam. "Are you still coming to the ranch next week?" Adam asked as Hailey tugged a toque on his head. "Mommy made your favorite chocolate cupcakes and put them in the freezer so me and Carter won't eat them."

"I'm excited for cupcakes," she said, hoping Dan didn't hear the waver in her voice.

Please, Lord, she prayed, *help me get over this. I don't want to feel so confused around him. This has to get easier.*

It's that whole first love thing, she reminded herself. You never really forget the drama and emotions of that first love. She just had to try.

Yet, as she wrapped Adam's scarf around his neck, she knew her reaction to Dan was beyond that of former high school sweethearts. Dan had been part of her dreams and the promise of a settled and secure future—something she had lacked with a mother who always wanted to be anywhere but Hartley Creek. And a father who had left her and her sisters long ago.

While she tied up the ends of the scarf, Adam turned his attention back to Dan.

"Are you Natasha's daddy?"

"Yes. Are you friends with her?" Dan asked back.

"I want to be, but she doesn't play with me. She's not fun."

Hailey tugged on Adam's scarf to get his attention. "Remember? We only say good things about our friends," she said, adding in a warning frown when Adam met her gaze.

"She's not my friend yet," Adam protested. "She won't play with me because all she does is cry."

She needed to work on the potency of her frown, Hailey thought. Obviously it had no effect on Adam. As Hailey glanced back at Dan she caught a shadow of pain cross his expression.

All week she and Megan had tried to be diplomatic with Dan in their discussions about Natasha. Dan kept insisting Natasha only needed a few more days to get used to the routine.

But Natasha needed more than a few more days to settle in. They hadn't told him yet that Natasha had spent all of today hunched over her knapsack, her hair hanging over her face, silent tears streaming down her cheeks.

Megan was saving that information for the parent-teacher meeting this afternoon.

Hailey pushed herself to her feet. "Out you go, buddy. Say hi to your mom and Carter for me," she said, sending Adam out the door, watching to make sure he got to the bus. When she saw the principal of the school urging Adam on, she turned back to Dan.

"So, how does that kid know your cousin Carter?" Dan asked.

"His mother, Emma, and my cousin Carter are engaged."

"Glad to hear that," Dan said, slipping his hands in the back pockets of his jeans. "Carter's had it pretty rough the past few years. What with losing his wife and then his little boy."

Hailey tried not to read too much into his knowledge of her family. Carter was her cousin, but he was also a part of the Hartley Creek community. Dan's mother and father would have kept Dan abreast of what was going on.

"Carter's happy now."

Dan nodded, then blew out a sigh. "What did that little guy mean when he said all Natasha does is cry?"

"Today wasn't a good day for Natasha." That was all she felt comfortable telling him.

"She'll have her good and bad days, I guess," Dan replied. The look he gave Hailey seemed to contain both challenge and hope.

She swallowed, unable to look away, wondering if he ever thought of their last time together and the fight they had. Had he done the same thing as she had done in the months that followed? Relive that conversation over and over? Say things differently?

After Austin died, Dan had pulled back. She had understood that and had given him room to grieve. Then, when he finally asked to get together again it was to tell her that he wanted to move away from Hartley Creek. When she asked him why he said only that he needed space.

As she'd faced him down, Hailey had relived the pain she felt when she'd watched her father silently pack his suitcase, then walk past her and out of the house. She had been eight years old then and vividly remembered her helplessness.

Added to the past memory was the reality that four months before Austin's accident, when Hailey had just graduated from high school, her mother, Denise, decided her youngest daughter was old enough to fend for herself. Her sisters, Naomi and Shannon, were out of the house already, so Denise packed up and moved away from Hartley Creek, leaving Hailey behind.

Then Dan wanted to leave her too?

It was all too much. This time she would be in charge, Hailey had thought. This time she wasn't going to be left behind. So she'd broken up with him.

Part of her had hoped, even yearned, that he would plead with her not to break up. That he would change his mind and want to stay in Hartley Creek with her.

But nothing.

The first six months he was gone, she nurtured the faint hope he would return. When she heard about his marriage to Lydia she knew their relationship had ended.

Though the sting of that betrayal had stayed with her a long time, the memory of the love she had held for him lingered.

And now, looking into his eyes, that old memory grew stronger and she was reluctantly drawn into his gaze.

She couldn't do this. Not here. Not now.

Relief flooded her when she saw Megan striding down the hall.

"Here's Miss Tolsma," she said, reaching blindly for the handle of the classroom door. "I'll sit with Natasha, until you're finished."

Then she turned and retreated into the room, closing the door firmly on Dan and on the past.

She'd found out the hard way the only way to stay in control of your own life was to stay in control of your plans.

No way was Dan disrupting them.

Chapter Two

Natasha sat in the little chair in the corner, still clutching her knapsack, her chin resting on the top of it, her brown hair hiding her face.

At least she wasn't crying anymore.

Hailey sat down beside her, perched awkwardly on a chair made for six-year-old bottoms. She folded her hands on her lap, saying nothing, simply being there for the little girl.

As if finally sensing her presence, Natasha looked up. Her red-rimmed eyes and tear-stained cheeks plucked at Hailey's heartstrings.

Natasha dragged her coat sleeve across her face, drying her eyes. "Is my daddy come yet?"

"He's talking to Miss Tolsma for a few minutes. As soon as they're done he'll come to get you."

"I want to be with my daddy. I don't want to be in this school." Natasha looked down at her knapsack, fiddling with a tiny stuffed rabbit hanging from the zipper pull.

"I'm sure your daddy wants to be with you too." Hailey laid her hand on Natasha's tiny shoulder.

Natasha shook her head. Hailey heard her draw in a trembling breath and her shoulders shook with silent sorrow, as if she had no hope her cries would be acknowledged.

Hailey's heart broke for the little girl adrift without her mother and living in an unfamiliar place.

"You know your daddy loves you very much," Hailey said, giving the little girl's hand a squeeze. "He wants to take very good care of you and he wants you to learn. That's why he put you in school."

Natasha's silent cries only increased. Hailey couldn't stand watching her. She pulled the little girl onto her lap. Natasha made a token protest, then wilted against Hailey, her arms twined around her neck.

Hailey wrapped her arms around the tiny, slender body, rocking slowly back and forth and making shushing noises. Natasha burrowed her head in Hailey's neck.

"I don't want to be sad," she murmured, sniffing.

"I know you miss your mom and this place is different. It's okay to be sad about that."

Natasha drew in a shuddering breath. "Daddy said I shouldn't talk about my mommy," she said. "Because it makes me cry."

Hailey felt torn. She didn't want to go against Dan's parenting, but she also wanted to look out for Natasha.

"You can talk about your mommy to me, if you want," Hailey said. "You can tell me anything you want about her."

Natasha considered this, then lay against Hailey again. "I really like you," she whispered.

"I like you too," Hailey replied, stroking Natasha's damp hair away from her face. She clung to the little girl. Dan's little girl.

What if Austin's accident hadn't happened? What if Dan had stayed in Hartley Creek? Would the little girl in her arms be her and Dan's?

The light touch of a hand on her shoulder made her jump. Hailey yanked herself back from her meandering thoughts, then just about fell off the chair when she turned and saw Dan pull his hand back from her.

A frown pulled his eyebrows together as he looked down at her.

"She was so upset...she was crying... I didn't know what to do." Hailey stumbled through her excuses, wondering why she felt she had to explain her behavior.

But Dan's direct gaze made her feel as if she had stepped over some invisible boundary.

He bent over and lifted Natasha away from Hailey and the little girl tucked herself into his arms. He stroked her hair just as Hailey had, tucking Natasha's head under his chin as he held her close.

Just as Hailey had.

"It's okay, honey," he murmured to his daughter. "We're making this better for you."

Hailey glanced over to Megan standing by the front doorway to the class, one arm crossed over her chest, her other hand tucked under her chin while she watched Dan and his little girl.

Hailey beat a retreat to her friend's side.

"Did you figure something out?" Hailey asked.

Megan ran her forefinger across her chin, as if drawing out her thoughts. Then she turned to Hailey. "We've decided that Natasha would do better with a tutor who could work with her in her home."

Hailey looked back to Dan, now perched on the edge of the small table, still holding his daughter.

"Good idea, but where will you find a tutor in Hartley Creek?" she asked, watching as Dan rocked slowly back and forth, comforting his daughter.

As a father has compassion on his children...

The Bible verse that had comforted her so often in the dark days following Austin's accident slipped into her mind.

Dan was a good father, so unlike her own.

Megan turned away from Dan to Hailey, lowering her voice. "I'm thinking this might be a good job for you."

Hailey's attention jerked away from Dan to her friend. "What, what?"

"Shush. Use your church voice," Megan whispered, holding her finger to her lips. "You and I both know that this little girl needs more help than any of the children in the classroom. When I saw you holding her on your lap, I knew you were exactly the right person for this job."

"I don't think so." She couldn't see Dan on a regular basis. That would put too heavy a strain on her emotions.

"But think of Natasha," Megan urged. "That little girl is overwrought. She recently lost her mother. She needs some kind of direction and she has obviously formed an attachment to you."

Hailey pressed her lips together as her sympathy for Natasha swayed her reasoning.

Megan sensed her wavering and put her hand on Hailey's shoulder. "I think you're exactly the right person for the job," she said.

Hailey shrugged, her reluctance battling with her sympathy for Natasha. "You can think all you want, but I'm sure Dan won't go for your plan."

"We'll see," was all Megan would say.

They walked over to where Dan sat, still holding Natasha. The little girl lay quietly in his arms.

Dan looked up when they came close, a raw hope in his eyes.

"I have a temporary solution to your problem." Megan

gave Dan a bright smile. "I've talked to Hailey about your situation and she is willing to tutor your daughter."

Dan's gaze flicked over Hailey and then returned to Megan. "I don't think that's an option," was his blunt response.

"I feel it's a reasonable solution," Megan replied, brushing aside his objections. "Hailey and Natasha obviously have some kind of bond."

Dan's only reply was to lift Natasha, stand up and settle her on his hip. Then he glanced over at Hailey. For a moment, as their eyes met, she caught a flicker of older emotions, a hearkening back to another time. Her heart faltered in response.

"This won't work," he said, then turned and walked away.

Hailey watched him leave, the definite tone in his voice cutting her to the core. Though Hailey had known Dan wouldn't agree, she didn't think he would be so adamant about it.

She wondered why she cared. Her response to him showed her she wasn't over Dan Morrow at all. And if she wasn't over Dan, she certainly shouldn't be teaching his daughter.

"Natasha, don't play with that, honey." Dan took the cardboard-and-cellophane box holding the baby doll away from his daughter.

It was Saturday afternoon and he and his mother had spent most of the day doing damage control, keeping his daughter from running up and down the aisles, fingering the china displays and playing with the toys in the store. Patricia, the store's only employee, manned the register.

"But it's pretty and I don't have a doll like that." Natasha stuck out her lip in a classic pout as she dropped onto the wooden floor, her green fairy dress puddling around her in a mass of glittery chiffon and satin.

Dan carefully closed the box and put it back up on the shelf with the rest of the toys. "Come with me to the front," he said, taking his daughter's hand. "Patricia said she has a game for you to play."

She jerked her hand away just as his cell phone rang out. Without bothering to check the caller, he pulled it from his pocket and answered it.

"We've been trying to call you for the past two days," a voice accused him.

At the sound of the woman's voice Dan's heart sank. Lydia's mother. Carla Anderson.

"I want the doll," Natasha called out, pulling away from Dan as he tried to control her and use his phone. Thankfully the store had hit a lull and Dan didn't have to deal with any customers right now.

"Is that Natasha?" Carla asked, her voice raising an octave. "What is wrong with her?"

"She's fine." The only thing wrong with her was she wasn't getting what she wanted. "And what can I do for you, Carla?" he asked, forcing himself to smile. He'd read somewhere that if you smile even if you don't feel like it, your voice sounds more pleasant. And he needed that pleasant tone right now. Every conversation with his mother-in-law since Lydia's death had been a battle over who would take care of Natasha. He had custody, but Lydia's parents brought it up at every turn.

In the weeks after Lydia's death Dan deliberately kept everyone out of his daughter's life just so he could cement his relationship with Natasha. He wanted to give her stability, create a connection. He'd had such little time with his daughter when Lydia was alive. However, in Dan's opinion that had meant keeping everyone, even his own parents, at arm's length for those first critical weeks after Lydia's death.

Now he lived in Hartley Creek and Carla and Alfred were still in Vancouver, and they'd been pushing harder and harder with each phone call.

"I want to talk to Natasha," Carla was saying. "I haven't talked to her for a couple of days."

Dan looked down at his sniffling daughter, then at the checkout counter. His mother was bagging some items for Miranda Klauer. The store was quiet, so he had time to supervise the phone call.

"Okay. I'll put her on," Dan said, as he took Natasha's hand and walked toward the door leading to his and Natasha's apartment above the store. They stepped into the stairwell and closed the door, leaving it open a crack so he could give them some privacy and yet keep an eye on what was going on outside.

"It's your gramma," he said to his daughter, lowering the phone and covering the mouthpiece. "She wants to talk to you. Do you want to talk to her?"

Natasha gave a halfhearted nod and Dan gave her the phone.

She lifted it, frowning just a bit, as if unsure what she would hear.

"Hi, Grandmother...I'm fine... Yes, I love my daddy. And he loves me." Natasha sat down on the first stair, fidgeting with a piece of her skirt as she listened to her grandmother. "My Gramma and Grandpa Deacon are really nice too.... It's cold here but I don't have to go to school." Natasha looked over at Dan, puzzlement crossing her features. "Because my daddy said so... My daddy can homeschool me, like my mommy did." Her frown deepened with each pause in the conversation as she listened to what her grandmother was saying. "But I like being with my daddy and I don't want to live with you—"

Fury rose up in Dan and he had to stop himself from snatching the phone away from Natasha. "I need to talk to Grandmother Anderson," he said, keeping his voice calm as he held out his hand.

Thankfully, Natasha willingly gave the phone up.

Dan took in a deep breath, then another, then raised the phone to his ear.

"We have all kinds of fun toys and I can take you to the park all the time because it's not cold here," Carla Anderson was saying.

"This is Dan." His words came out clipped and he didn't bother smiling this time. "What are you doing?"

A pause greeted his angry question, then Carla cleared her throat. "I was merely pointing out to Natasha the advantages of residing with us. And I think they are numerous."

Dan massaged the bridge of his nose, praying for patience, praying he didn't lose it in front of Natasha, who was watching him from her perch on the stair.

"We are not having this discussion now." He pitched his voice low, hoping he sounded nonthreatening. Hoping the fear twisting his gut didn't come out in his voice.

He'd spent almost six years of Natasha's short life battling with his ex-wife to get her to respect Dan's court-ordered weekend visits with his daughter. He had struggled not to run to court every time Lydia had decided this weekend she might take Natasha out of town, or Natasha was too sick to come, or any other lame excuse. He didn't want Natasha to become a pawn in their battle. But it had been difficult not to succumb when a month could go by with no visit.

Sad as Lydia's death had been, in one way, for Dan, it

had been a relief from the constant tension of battling over visits with his daughter.

Then, shortly after the funeral, he'd received a phone call from Lydia's brother, a lawyer, warning Dan that his parents wanted to sue for custody of Natasha. Since then the battle lines had been drawn and Mr. and Mrs. Anderson had slowly advanced, revealing their strategy one methodical step at a time.

The past few days their tactic had been to convince Natasha she wanted to live with them.

"We're not giving up on Natasha." Carla warned. "We have much to give her."

Dan bit back an angry reply. Mr. and Mrs. Anderson owned a condo in Hawaii, a twenty-six-foot yacht anchored in the Victoria Harbor, a small private plane and a home just outside of Vancouver with more square footage than both his parents' hardware store and the grocery store beside it.

"She's my daughter," he said, "and I will take care of her."

"That may be, but she said she's not going to school. How is that taking care of her?"

Dan should have known Carla wouldn't have missed one beat in Natasha's conversation. "She's having a hard time adjusting." No sooner had the words left his lips than he felt like banging his head on the wall behind him. Why give them any kind of ammunition? What kind of idiot was he?

"You do realize your daughter needs to attend school. That is still required," Carla replied, a note of triumph in her voice.

The all-too-familiar panic rose up in him as he felt himself backed into a corner. He glanced over at Natasha. She was smiling at him, rocking back and forth on the stair. He wasn't letting her go. Never.

Mrs. Anderson was still talking. "If you aren't responsible enough to take care of her schooling, perhaps we will have to—"

"I'm getting a tutor," he snapped, cutting her off midthreat. He leaned back against the wall behind him, the old cliché of being stuck between a rock and a hard place suddenly becoming very real. Could he hire Hailey? See her every day?

Maybe there was another way. Someone else to tutor Natasha.

"I see." Mrs. Anderson's clipped tone showed him that he had, for now, caused her to retreat. "Then I guess we'll have to see how things pan out for her."

"Yes, we will." Dan experienced a momentary reprieve and, to his disappointment, one of his knees began to bounce, an involuntary reaction to stress. He pushed it down and forced a smile that came more naturally this time. "And now I'm saying goodbye." He ended the call before Mrs. Anderson could ask to speak to Natasha again.

He laid his head back against the wall, closing his eyes.

"Are you tired, Daddy?" Natasha asked him, tugging on his hand.

He looked down at her, feeling the weight of his responsibilities. He *was* tired. Tired of trying to balance all the emotions his homecoming had created. Tired of trying to do it all himself.

In spite of what he had told Natasha's grandmother, however, he wasn't sure he was ready to have Hailey tutor his daughter every day. Surely he could find someone else to do the job.

"No, honey. I'm fine." He dropped his phone in his pocket and took her hand. "Now, let's go see if Gramma needs any help."

Hailey smoothed her hair, pressed her lips together and then caught herself mid-preen as she walked out of the cloakroom. *It's church, silly. And like last week, Dan won't be here anyway.*

In spite of her self-chiding, she still tugged on the wide leather belt cinching her knit dress, pressed her lips together to even out her lipstick, then threaded her way through the people gathered in the foyer, toward the doors leading to the sanctuary.

She paused in the doorway, glancing around the church, looking for a place to sit. Shannon was working at the hospital this morning and her Nana wanted to sleep in, so neither of them would be here this morning.

She caught sight of her cousin Carter's dark head bent over his fiancée, Emma, her son, Adam, sitting on his lap. People sat on either side of them, so it didn't look like there was room for her there.

"Miss Deacon. Miss Deacon," Natasha's voice called out over the buzz of conversation from the lobby. Hailey's heart skipped its next beat.

She turned to see Dan's tall figure moving through the people gathered in the foyer. His dark blond hair still glistened with moisture, as if he had stepped right out of the shower, gotten dressed and come here. As Natasha pulled him closer she also saw a line of blood trickling from a cut on his cheek. Probably shaved as quickly as he had dressed.

"Miss Deacon, you come to church too?" Natasha asked, beaming with pleasure.

"Yes. I do." Hailey returned her smile, yet couldn't stop her eyes from drifting toward Dan.

He wore a blue blazer over a light blue shirt. No tie, and jeans with cowboy boots. Just as he always did. And just as before, one point of his collar was tucked under the lapel of his blazer and the other lay overtop.

Hailey had to stop herself from reaching out to straighten it. As she always did.

"Hello, Hailey," he said.

Hailey hoped her smile looked as polite and emotionless as his. Then she noticed the trickle of blood heading dangerously close to his collar.

"You're bleeding," Hailey said, pointing to his face.

Dan grimaced and lifted his hand to the wrong cheek. Without thinking Hailey pulled a tissue out of her purse and pressed it to his face. She felt the warmth of his cheek through the tissue.

Dan, however, pulled back, smearing the blood.

"Sorry. So sorry," she said, angry at how breathless she sounded. "It's just the blood was going to stain the collar of your shirt. I thought I should stop it. I didn't mean—"

Stop now, she chastised herself as she handed him the tissue again.

He took it from her and slowly wiped his cheek. "I should go to the washroom and clean this up," he said. "Would you mind watching Natasha for me?" he asked.

Hailey gave a tight shake of her head, pulling her gaze away from him. She drew in a long, careful breath. *Please Lord, help me through this,* she prayed. *I'll be seeing him from time to time. Just let me get my silly emotions settled down.*

As Dan left, Natasha caught Hailey's hand in hers, clinging to it. "I wanted to wear my fairy wings to church so I could look like an angel, but my Daddy said I couldn't."

Hailey dragged her attention from Dan's retreating back to the little girl.

Natasha swung Hailey's hand as if they had known each other for years instead of only a few days.

"I think you look like an angel now," Hailey returned.

"I don't like this dress, but my daddy said I had to wear it." Natasha pulled at the dress, her blue cotton tied at the waist. White tights and black patent leather shoes finished the look.

"You look really nice," Hailey said, but from the look of Natasha's sloppy ponytail she suspected Dan hadn't had much luck with her hair.

"My daddy said we had to hurry to get to church so we could sit with Gramma and Grandpa, but I want to sit with you," Natasha said, looking up at Hailey.

"You better wait to see what your daddy says," Hailey returned. Knowing the tension surrounding them each time they got together, she doubted Dan would give in to that request.

People moved past, smiling at her and Natasha. A few stopped to chat, but most walked directly into the sanctuary. Finally Dan appeared again. The cut on his cheek was only a tiny red line and seemed to have stopped bleeding.

Without looking at her, Dan reached for Natasha's hand. "We should go, sweetie," he said.

But Natasha wouldn't let go of Hailey. "I want to sit with Miss Deacon."

"I'm sure Miss Deacon has her own place to sit," he said, motioning her forward.

But Natasha wouldn't move.

Hailey saw Dan press his lips together and tried to release Natasha's death grip on her own fingers. "You should go with your daddy," she said.

Natasha's lips thinned and she gave a quick shake of her head as she gave Hailey a determined look. "I want to sit with you." Her voice rose on that last word and people already seated in the sanctuary were looking back at them. Some looked concerned, some grinned, and Hailey sensed Dan's growing frustration.

Dan tried one more time to take Natasha away.

"I want to be with Miss Deacon," she called out as Dan took her hand firmly in his.

A few more heads turned and a few titters flew around the sanctuary. And in case neither Dan nor Hailey understood Natasha's determination, she emphasized her little pique with a stamp of her foot.

Hailey looked over Natasha's head at Dan. "I don't mind if you and her sit with me," she said, giving him a gracious way to give in to Natasha.

Dan drummed his fingers on his thigh, then gave a reluctant nod of his head. "Okay. I guess we can."

In spite of the tension of the moment Hailey couldn't stop a tiny frisson of pleasure at the thought of sitting with him. She dragged her attention back to Natasha. "I guess we'll need to find an empty spot," she said to the little girl. Then without another glance at Dan, she turned and walked down the aisle, searching for a place near the back where they wouldn't be too obvious.

As they passed Carter and Emma, she caught Carter looking at her and Natasha. Hailey averted her glance, but not soon enough to miss the smirk on her cousin's face. A flush heated her cheeks, but she kept her head up and finally found a spot at the end of a pew. Hailey slipped into the empty space, Natasha right behind her. And Dan right behind Natasha.

Hailey settled into the pew and, as Natasha slipped her arm into hers, tried not to look over at Dan. Thankfully the service started and the first song was announced. Hailey reached for the songbook at the same time as Dan. As their fingers brushed, she pulled her own hand back, curling her fingers against her palm.

Dan simply opened the book to the correct page and held it out for her to follow along.

Please help me get through this service, she prayed as she folded her hands together and sang along. *Please help me to stay focused on You, Lord, and not be distracted by Dan.*

When the song was over Hailey sat down and kept her gaze forward, concentrating on the worship team. The pastor. Anything but the man sitting a couple of feet away.

Natasha leaned contentedly against Hailey, swinging her feet back and forth, her arm tucked in Hailey's. By the time the pastor started preaching, however, Hailey felt Natasha's body grow heavier and heard her breathing slow.

She shot a quick glance down at the girl, surprised to see her eyes closed. Dan seemed to have noticed too. He reached over to take her from Hailey, but even in her sleep, Natasha clung to Hailey, shifted, then laid her head on Hailey's lap.

Hailey looked down at the little girl's face, so relaxed and innocent in sleep. Her heart faltered and she couldn't stop her hand from lightly brushing the child's hair back from her face, then letting her hand rest on Natasha's shoulder. She looked over at Dan at the same time he looked at her, and in his eyes she caught a fleeting glimpse of sadness. *It's not my fault,* she wanted to say, as she did not understand the strange attachment the young girl seemed to have to her.

Dan held her gaze a moment, then looked down at Natasha. He reached over and put his hand on her arm, as if laying his own claim to the little girl.

The service flowed on and still Natasha slept, her

warmth and vulnerability creating a surprising feeling of protectiveness in Hailey.

But, to her shame, in spite of focusing her attention on the pastor, she was far too aware of Dan's hand resting only inches from hers.

Chapter Three

The chords of the last song rang through the sanctuary and Dan waited a moment, too many emotions storming the defenses he'd spent seven years putting in place.

All through the service he'd been far too conscious of Hailey. Her movements. The way she would curl her hair around her finger. The way she would smile at a point the minister had made.

Sometimes it seemed that the past seven years were just a drift of smoke, but then all he had to do was look at his daughter and realize that, between him and Hailey, everything had changed.

Now, as Natasha lay with her head on Hailey's lap, part of him wanted to snatch Natasha away from Hailey, pull his little girl to himself. Pull himself into the present.

But part of him also felt a disturbing sense of rightness. Hailey had always wanted to be a mother. She had always talked about having a large family. Six kids. Maybe more.

Dan gave himself a mental shake, erasing past emotions and history that had come back to haunt the present. What he felt for Hailey didn't belong here and now.

However, right now he had another reality to deal with. Natasha's schooling.

Hailey gently shook Natasha, trying to wake her up, but she wouldn't even open her eyes.

Dan sat down again. "Just leave her," he said quietly. "I need to talk to you anyway." He glanced over his shoulder at the people leaving the sanctuary. He couldn't see his parents, which was just as well. He needed a moment with Hailey. Alone.

As he waited, the buzz of conversation from the exiting congregation was punctuated with bursts of laughter. Light streamed over the emptying pews from the stained glass windows, bathing everyone in a multicolored glow.

Not much had changed here, he thought.

"What do you want to talk to me about?" Hailey asked, shooting him a puzzled frown.

Dan didn't say anything right away. In a few moments they could speak in private. Finally, the last people left the foyer and only then did Dan turn to Hailey.

"I have a favor to ask of you," he said, keeping his voice low so he wouldn't wake Natasha.

"Sure. What is it?"

Dan tapped his fingers on the back of the wooden pew, realizing how silly he was about to look, given his initial resistance to Hailey tutoring his daughter.

But that was before the in-laws' phone call. Before the pressure to come up with a solution had pushed him to this place. Before he had realized there was no one else to do the job.

"I was wondering if you're still willing to tutor Natasha," he said.

"What? Why now?"

Dan pursed his lips, trying to think of how to tell her, then decided to go with the easiest response. The truth.

"Ever since Lydia died, her parents have been pushing to get custody of Natasha. When they found out she wasn't going to school, they saw it as ammunition." He couldn't stop the bitter tone that crept into his voice. Or the anger. He paused a moment to settle himself, then looked over at Hailey. "Truth is, I'm stuck. I need a tutor, and because you're a qualified teacher, that makes it easier to prove I'm doing the right thing with Natasha's schooling." He didn't add that he couldn't find anyone else.

Before Hailey's glance slid away from him, he caught a glimpse of pain in her gray eyes.

He didn't want to analyze why she might feel that way. He felt as if he was using her, but when it came to his daughter he would do anything.

"I'll pay you," he added, hoping, praying she wouldn't turn him down. "I don't expect you to do this for free."

Hailey raised her hand as if to say stop. "Don't worry about that. I'll tutor her."

The tension in Dan's shoulders released. "Great. I appreciate that. I will pay you, though. At least as much as you're making at the school."

Hailey gently stroked Natasha's hair. Dan was surprised to see a slight tremor in her fingers. "Did you want me to start tomorrow?" she asked.

"That would be best."

Hailey pulled in a long, slow breath, then turned back to him. "Are you sure about this?"

Her direct question accentuated his own concerns but he knew he had no choice.

"I have to be," was all he could say to her.

Her eyes held his and in her expression he saw all the misgivings he also had entertained.

It would work, he told himself. A lot had happened between then and now. They were different people now.

Besides, it was only for a while. Once Natasha had eased

back into regular classroom life, he wouldn't need Hailey's help anymore.

And once the school year was over, Hailey would be leaving Hartley Creek anyway.

"Are you sure it's a good idea to be tutoring Dan's girl?" Shannon closed a cupboard door in her kitchen and set a bowl beside the stove. "That won't be awkward?" Hailey's sister tossed her long, wavy hair away from her face as she dumped a pan of green beans into the bowl. Then she reached past Hailey for the nutmeg.

Hailey blew out a sigh as she carved up the chicken for the dinner she and Shannon were preparing for Nana in Shannon's apartment. "Hopefully not. I mean we're both adults. Besides, when he married Lydia he made it clear he had moved on."

"But still—"

"Have you heard anything more from Naomi?" Hailey didn't want to talk about her and Dan's past. She had shed enough tears over Dan's decisions and Shannon had been witness to most of them. Hailey had her own life now and Dan wasn't a part of it. "Last I talked to her, the oncologist said Billy had maybe another month?"

Shannon shook her head. "Poor Naomi. When she and Billy got engaged, who could have imagined this would happen?"

"Do you think she'll be back for Carter and Emma's wedding?"

"I hope so." Shannon frowned as she sprinkled nutmeg over the bowl of steaming beans. "Our poor sister has had to deal with so much, it would be good for her to be around family."

"Hopefully Garret will be done with that engineering job in Dubai by then."

"I hope so too. I'm looking forward to having everyone back for a while."

"What do you mean, for a while?" Nana Beck's quiet voice interrupted the sisters' conversation. She settled herself in the folding chair beside the plastic table that took up one corner of Shannon's minuscule kitchen.

"You know I have a teaching job in Calgary come September," Hailey said, laying a drumstick on the plate she was filling up.

"I still don't believe you can't find a job closer to home," Nana complained.

Hailey gave her grandmother a placating smile. "Calgary is only a three-hour drive away. I'll be back to visit."

Nana smoothed back her gray hair. "At least I've got three of my grandchildren together for now. And Carter seems so happy now that he and Emma are making their wedding plans."

"Yeah. Lucky Carter." Hailey felt truly happy for her cousin, but Dan's return to town reminded her of her own might-have-beens.

"You'll find someone, don't worry," Nana assured her, as if she could read her granddaughter's mind. "Maybe in Calgary. Or maybe here. Now that Dan Morrow is back. You two were such a sweet couple."

Hailey caught Shannon's sympathetic glance at their grandmother's lack of subtlety. Her sister, more than anyone, knew exactly how much Dan's desertion had hurt her.

"Lots of other fish in the sea, Nana," Shannon said. "And sometimes you need to try another sea."

Nana Beck sighed at that. "Well, I keep praying for all you grandchildren. That you will all make better choices than my daughters did. That you will make the kind of choice your great-great-grandfather August Beck did."

Shannon walked over to their grandmother and dropped a light kiss on her forehead. "That means a lot to us, Nana." She gave her grandmother the bowl of beans. "Why don't you put this on the table in the dining room and when Hailey is finished butchering that chicken, we can eat."

"I've got things under control," Hailey protested, even as she struggled to cut the breast away from the bone.

Shannon put her hand on Hailey's shoulder and gave her a knowing look. "I sure hope so, little sister."

Hailey caught the questioning subtext in her sister's comment and looked away.

She sure hoped she had things under control. Seeing Dan every day would create a challenge to keeping her heart whole.

But she had to. She just had to keep thinking of leaving Hartley Creek and starting over in a new job in a new city. It was the only way she would get through the next few months.

Hailey shifted her backpack on her shoulder, then took the first steps up the flight of wooden stairs hugging the brick wall at the back of Hartley Creek Hardware Store. A cutting winter wind whistled around her ears and through the open zipper of her down-filled jacket. She wrested the sides of her coat together, as memories emerged with each step up the stairs.

When she and Dan were dating they would take turns doing homework at each other's place. When her mother was gone, which was frequently, Hailey would come to Dan's place. They would sit beside each other, papers spread over the table, a plate of fresh-baked cookies in front of them.

Mostly, though, she and Dan would just hold hands

under the table and whisper to each other. They would make up scenarios and weave plans.

Dan would become a partner with his father in the store. Hailey would work at the ski hill until the kids came.

Hailey's steps faltered as she made her way up the stairs, her hand clinging to the wooden rail.

Okay, Lord. I know doing this will bring up many memories, but that's long over. Done. We were just kids then. We've both moved on to different places. We're both different people. Please help me remember that.

She waited a moment, as if to give the prayer time to wing its way upward, then she followed it up the rest of the stairs. She rapped on the door, then hugged her coat around her, glancing over her shoulder at the mountains surrounding the town.

From here she could barely make out the The Shadow Woman. The contours of her face and body would show up better in the latter part of summer and even more clearly from just the right spot on Carter's ranch, the old family place.

Melancholy drifted through her. By August, she would be leaving Hartley Creek.

The creak of the door opening made her turn around.

Once again, Dan stood in front of her. She caught the piney scent of his aftershave, the same one he always wore. The kind she had bought him when he'd started shaving.

His hair, still damp from the shower, curled a bit. He wore it shorter than he used to but the look suited his strong features and deep-set eyes.

"Hey," was all he said, adding a curt nod. "Natasha will be right out. She's cleaning up her bedroom."

He stepped aside for Hailey to come in and as she looked around the apartment, she felt the brush of nostalgia. Her eyes flitted over the gray recliner, the overstuffed green couch and love seat, all facing the television perched on a worn wooden stand. Beyond that, through the arched doorway to the dining room, she saw the same heavy wooden table and matching chairs with their padded brocade seats.

The same pictures still hung on the walls, the same knick-knacks filled the bookshelf along one wall of the living room.

"Looks like your parents still live here," she said, dropping her backpack on the metal table in the front hallway and removing her jacket.

"Mom and Dad wanted a fresh start when they moved out," Dan said, reaching for her coat. "They took only a few things to the new house."

As Dan took her coat, their fingers brushed. Just a light touch, inconsequential in any other circumstance, with any other person. Trouble was, Dan wasn't just any other person.

Just as she had at church yesterday, she jerked her hand back, wrapping it around the other. "You probably want to get back to work." Thankfully, her voice sounded brisk and businesslike, betraying none of the emotions that arose in his presence.

"Mom and Patricia have been downstairs for half an hour already," Dan said as he hung her coat up in the cupboard beside the door. "I need to get going."

Hailey nodded as she picked up her backpack with the assignments Megan had planned for Natasha. "I imagine the dining room is the best place to work."

"That's what I thought." Dan shifted his feet, his hands in the front pockets of his pants, and Hailey wondered if the same memories of their past slipped through his mind. "I just want to tell you I appreciate you coming here. I know it keeps you from helping Megan."

"I'm sure Natasha will be back at school in no time," Hailey said with a breeziness she didn't quite feel. "So Megan won't be without my help for long."

"I hope so. I'll get Natasha." Dan took a step back and then headed down the long, narrow hallway just off the living room.

She ambled over the worn carpet, then through the arched doorway to the dining room. The table was cleared off and she set her knapsack down on its polished wooden surface. Hailey zipped open the knapsack, glancing around as she pulled out her papers and books. The glass-fronted armoire in the dining room still held the same plates, tea-cups and serving bowls. Why had Mrs. Morrow left so much behind?

Then Hailey's eyes fell on the row of school photographs marching along the facing wall.

Pictures of Dan ranged from a pudgy, freckle-faced kin-dergartner with a gap-toothed grin to the serious senior. Already in grade twelve he showed a hint of the man he had now become, with his deep-set eyes and strong chin.

Hailey was surprised at the little lift his pictures gave her. At the memories they evoked.

She turned her attention to the row of pictures below Dan's. Austin's narrow features grinned back at her from the school photos, his blue eyes sparkling with the mischief that typified his outlook on life, the complete opposite of his older, more serious brother.

But Austin's series ended with a photograph from grade eleven. The year he died. Regret for might-have-beens twisted her stomach, then she turned, putting the pictures behind her.

"Miss Deacon, you came." The bright voice of Natasha banished the memory. As the little girl bounded into the room, her brown hair bounced behind her.

Today Natasha wore a lime-green T-shirt tucked into torn blue jeans. A pair of sparkly yellow angel wings completed the look.

Obviously the little girl had chosen some of her own clothes today.

"Wow. Don't you look spiffy," Hailey said, trying not to smile too hard at her ensemble.

"These are my favorite wings," Natasha announced as she lifted the wand in her hand and performed an awkward twirl, almost knocking over a plant stand in the process.

"Natasha, please, no dancing in the house," Dan said, catching the rocking houseplant and setting it out of reach of her wings. "I'd like you to go take off your fairy wings."

Quick as a flash Natasha's good mood morphed into a sullen glare. "I like my wings and you said I couldn't wear them to school. But this isn't school."

"This is *like* school," Dan said, kneeling down in front of her. "And I want you to behave for Miss Deacon."

Natasha caught the end of her hair and twirled it around her finger, her attention on the books on the table and not on what her father was saying. "Are those mine?" she asked.

"Yes. They are." Hailey glanced at her watch. "And it's almost time for us to start."

"But first the fairy wings come off," Dan insisted.

"I want to keep them on," she protested, wiggling away from him.

Dan cradled her face in his hands and turned her to face him. "Sorry, honey, but now it's time for school, not time for pretending. Now I have to go to work and you have to stay up here, but I'll be back at lunchtime, okay?"

Natasha pouted but then it seemed the fight went out of her. "Okay, Daddy. But you'll be right downstairs, won't you?"

Dan nodded, tucking a tangle of hair behind her ear. Then he brushed a gentle kiss over her forehead. "Love you, munchkin," he said as he slipped the wings off her shoulders.

"Love you, punchkin," she repeated with a giggle.

Dan set the wings aside and smoothed her hair again, smiling at her, the love for his daughter softening his features.

Hailey swallowed as she watched the scene between them. She always knew Dan would make a good father.

Her heart twisted a moment with old sorrow and old regrets and a flurry of other questions. Why had Dan married Lydia? Why had he moved on so quickly from her to another woman?

She pressed her eyes shut a moment, as if to close her mind to the past.

It was none of her business, she reminded herself.

And it was a bleak reminder that what she and Dan had was dead and gone.

Chapter Four

"I don't want to do math now. I hate math." Natasha pushed her chair away from the table, the wooden legs screeching over the worn linoleum. She folded her arms over her chest as she pushed out her lower lip.

For the past hour Hailey had been working with Natasha on math problems and all they had to show for the time were some princess doodles on the bottom of the page and one measly solved problem. Which made Hailey wonder how much homeschooling Lydia had done.

"Don't say hate. Say instead that you don't *like* math," Hailey corrected, picking up the pencil Natasha had tossed on the table. "We want to save the word *hate* for really big things."

Natasha shot her a puzzled glance. "What big things?"

Hailey held the pencil out to Natasha, waiting for her to take it. "Big things like sin and killing and saying bad things about God."

Natasha pursed her lips, as if pondering this, then tossed her brown hair over her shoulder and took the pencil from Hailey.

"My mommy said there's no such thing as God," Natasha said, doodling a princess in one corner of the paper.

Hailey wasn't sure what to say as she watched Natasha add a crown to the princess's head. She didn't want to disparage Natasha's memory of her mother, but she was fairly sure Dan disagreed with Lydia's beliefs. He'd always had a strong faith in God. At least he had until the day of Austin's death.

Natasha wiggled a bit, then put her pencil down. "I have to go the bathroom," she said, slipping off her chair before Hailey could stop her.

Hailey let her go. Finding routine would take time with a little girl who didn't seem to know the meaning of the word.

As Hailey gathered up the pencils Natasha had scattered over the table, her eyes were drawn to the pictures on the wall of Austin and Dan.

She drew in a long, slow breath, stifling the painful memories resurrected by Austin's face. So easily she remembered the day Austin died.

The three of them, Dan, Hailey and Austin, had been snowboarding together. Hailey had gotten separated from Dan and Austin in the lineup for the chairlift and, by the time she got to the top of the hill, only Dan was waiting for her. He told her that Austin had gone off on his own.

Dan and Hailey had spent most of the afternoon on the runs at the top of the mountain, and they got to the bottom only to find out that Austin had gone out of bounds on a black diamond run and had gone over a rocky ledge.

He had died instantly.

And right after that Dan and Hailey's relationship had fallen apart.

"I'm done," Natasha announced, coming back to the room.

The little girl's voice broke into the thoughts flashing through Hailey's mind. She pulled her hands over her face as if wiping them away. She needed to get out of this apartment and the memories it evoked. And from the way Natasha had been struggling to concentrate the past hour, she needed to go out too.

Hailey made a quick decision.

"You know what we're going to do?" Hailey asked, gathering up the papers and the pencils. "We're going to do some schoolwork downstairs."

Natasha jumped up eagerly, then frowned. "My daddy said he doesn't want me in the store. He said I make problems."

"I'll be with you." Hailey picked up a folder and slipped the papers inside.

"But my daddy—" Natasha protested again.

"I'll talk to your daddy and help him to understand," Hailey said with more assurance than she felt.

All morning the little girl had been unable to concentrate on even the simplest problems. Maybe a different method of teaching was in order. And Hailey had just the idea of how this was to be done.

"First I have to put on my wings," Natasha said.

Hailey didn't bother to stop her. One step at a time, she reminded herself.

A few moments later, wings firmly in place, she and Natasha were headed down the narrow stairs inside the apartment leading to the store below.

"We have to be quiet," Hailey whispered. "We don't want your daddy to get angry with us."

Hailey pushed open the door and was greeted by the buzz of conversation and the chiming of the cash register as Dan's mother rang up another sale.

The wooden floor creaked under her feet as she and Natasha crept toward the bins at the back of the store, where Hailey knew they wouldn't be in anyone's way. She couldn't see Patricia or Dan. So far, so good.

"The Makita is a good choice," she heard Dan's deep voice say on the other side of the aisle. "You won't regret it."

"That's my daddy," Natasha called out and pulled her hand free before Hailey could stop her. Natasha's glittery wings bounced as she jogged down the aisle. As she rounded the corner, one wing caught the edge of a toolbox and stopped her headlong rush. As Natasha lost her balance, the box toppled toward her and knocked her over. She sat a moment, looking shocked, and then her wounded cries reverberated through the store.

"Natasha. What are you doing here? Where's Miss Deacon?"

Hailey caught up to Natasha at the same time as Dan, not surprised at the suppressed anger in his voice. Hailey pulled the box off Natasha and Dan pulled his now-sobbing daughter up into his arms. He brushed her tangled hair off her face, looking her over as she kept crying.

"I think she's more scared than hurt," Hailey said over Natasha's wails, trying to put the box back on the shelf.

"What is she doing down here?" Dan asked as he tucked Natasha's head against his neck. Then, behind Dan, Hailey caught the curious glance of the customer Dan had been helping. Great. Carter's gray eyes sparkled with mischief and the smirk on her cousin's face told her that whatever happened here would be reported posthaste to Nana, her sister Shannon and Carter's fiancée, Emma.

"Thanks for the help, Dan," Carter said. "I'll go pay for this."

"Let me know how that drill works out for you," Dan replied, the scowl on his face showing Hailey how bothered he was at this interruption.

Carter winked at Hailey, then left, his cowboy boots echoing on the wooden floor.

"So why are you here?" Dan set Natasha on the floor, his scowl deepening. "I hired you so I wouldn't have to deal with these kinds of distractions."

"Natasha has been having difficulty staying focused, so I thought we could try some hands-on problem solving." Hailey strived to sound as though she was in control of the situation.

"I thought your job was to get her to stay focused?" Dan growled.

Hailey put on her most pleasant expression and nodded. "This is a transition time."

Dan's hazel eyes narrowed. "I still don't see how bringing her down here and disrupting things will help her."

Hailey forced herself to stay calm and not get pulled into the challenge she saw in his gaze. "I'll make sure she stays out of your way and doesn't bother customers. It's just for a few moments, to give her a bit of a break."

Dan shook his head. "I prefer if you keep her upstairs. She has to learn to stay on task. That's what I hired you for."

"You also hired me to use my judgment, right?" She forced a smile, hoping she didn't sound as contrary as she felt.

Dan didn't return her smile. "I hired you to do what I want. Right now I want you to take her upstairs and work with her there. Goofing around in the store won't help her make the transition."

He held her gaze a beat, as if to reinforce what he'd said.

Though every part of her rebelled, Hailey guessed this was not the time and place to argue with him.

Natasha pulled on her hand. "Can we go do my schoolwork now?"

Lowering her shoulders Hailey took a deep breath to relax. She'd have to find a better time to have this discussion with Dan. But they would have it. He had hired her to do a job and if he didn't like her methods, then he would have to find someone else.

"We're going back upstairs, sweetie," Hailey said, putting her hands on Natasha's shoulders.

"I don't like it in the 'partment. I want to be here with my daddy."

Well, your daddy doesn't want you to be here with him.

Hailey knew that wasn't entirely true. Dan had his own ideas of how Natasha should be schooled but, unfortunately, they didn't coincide with hers.

"I like this sandwich." Natasha grinned as she looked up from the plate Hailey had set in front of her. "How did you make it look like a rabbit?"

"Your grandmother has a great big cookie cutter in the shape of a rabbit," Hailey said. She remembered when Dan's mother had brought the cookie cutter up from the store. Dan and Austin had teased Mrs. Morrow about the humongous cookies she would be making with them and how fat they would all get eating rabbit cookies.

The memory teased up other emotions, which she fought down with a sense of dismay. Was this how it would be for the rest of her time teaching Natasha? Old memories and old emotions constantly assaulting her?

She took a quick breath. Just get through it.

"Aren't you making a sandwich?" Natasha asked, swinging her feet as she picked up her rabbit.

"Not for me. I'm going to eat with some friends at a café," Hailey said, just as the stairway door creaked open.

Dan stepped into the apartment, talking on his cell

phone. "I needed that order yesterday," he said as he bent over Natasha's head and gave her a kiss.

When Hailey got back from the kitchen with the sandwich she had made for him, he had finished his phone call.

"How was your morning, munchkin?" Dan asked, sitting down beside Natasha as Hailey set a plate in front of him. "Did you get lots of work done?"

"I got bored and then I got sad." Natasha delivered the comment with a sorrowful look Dan's way, and just in case he didn't get that, she added a dramatic sniff.

"What were you sad about?"

"My mommy."

Dan pulled the corner of his lip between his teeth, then pointed to the plate in front of her. "But look at the cool sandwich Miss Deacon made for you. It looks like…a rabbit?" He shot Hailey a puzzled look.

"I used that old cookie cutter of your mother's."

"She still has it around?" Dan's mouth quirked up in a grin, which didn't help Hailey's equilibrium around him. She'd thought he would still be upset with her for taking Natasha downstairs. It appeared she'd been forgiven.

"I thought it would make her sandwich more interesting," Hailey returned, wrapping her purple sweater around herself. "So, if you guys are good, I'm heading down to Mug Shots for lunch."

Dan's puzzled expression held a touch of relief. The awkwardness between them was palpable and she guessed he would be more comfortable if she left.

"Sure. Thanks a lot for the sandwich. You didn't have to do that."

"I didn't mind," Hailey said, walking to the cupboard to get her coat.

"No. You can't go," Natasha cried out. "You have to stay

and eat with us. Daddy always says it's important to eat together."

Hailey gave the little girl a gentle smile as she pulled her coat on. "Your dad was talking about families eating together," she said, pulling her hair free from the collar. "Which you are doing right now. You and your daddy are a family."

Natasha turned to Dan, grabbing his arm and giving it a tug. "Tell her she has to stay. Tell her, Daddy."

Conflicting emotions flitted across Dan's features.

Hailey held up her hand, forestalling his answer and giving him an out. "No. I should go. I have some friends waiting for me I want to visit with." Not entirely true, but there was bound to be someone she knew hanging around Mug Shots.

As she zipped up her jacket, Dan's cell phone rang.

Dan answered it, then, as he spoke, glanced up at Hailey, frowning. "Yeah, I guess I can," he said. He ended the call, then eased out a sigh as he held her eyes. "That was Jess Schroder. I need to meet him down at the lumberyard in twenty minutes."

Hailey bit her lip as she checked the clock. "That doesn't give me enough time to get to the coffee shop, eat and come back." She hesitated a moment more, then accepted the inevitable. "I guess I better eat lunch here," she said, unzipping her coat.

"Sorry about that," Dan said. "I'll make sure you get a break tomorrow."

She just nodded, then returned to the kitchen to make a sandwich for herself. She took her time, not sure she wanted to sit down at the table with Dan and Natasha. The situation smacked of domesticity.

She brought her sandwich to the table, sat down, then bowed her head, her hair falling like a curtain around her

flushed cheeks. *Dear Lord, just help me get through this,*
she prayed. *Help me act around Dan like I would around
any other guy. And bless this food, please, and thanks for
all the blessings I have.*

She waited a moment, as if to let the prayer settle. When
she looked up she caught Dan's enigmatic expression. She
knew what he was thinking. At one time church, God and
praying had not figured prominently in her life.

I'm not the irresponsible and goofy girl I used to be, she
wanted to say.

Though she kept her thoughts to herself, she was unable
to look away, unable to stop the tender stirring in her chest
of older emotions. Older attractions.

"Why were you looking at your sandwich?" Natasha
asked.

Hailey broke the connection, smiling at Natasha's confusion. "I was praying a blessing on my food."

"Why?" Natasha pressed, biting off the ear of her bunny
sandwich.

Hailey cut her bread in two, then carefully laid her knife
down, considering her answer. "It's because everything we
have comes from God and so does our food. So I like to
thank Him for it."

"How come we don't do that, Daddy?"

"Because I don't always think of it," was his quiet response. "But we should."

Hailey kept her attention on her sandwich, perplexed
at the change in their situation. At one time she'd been the
one who didn't pray and seldom went to church. Now, it
seemed, Dan was the one who had moved away from the
faith he'd been raised with.

"My mommy never prayed either," Natasha was saying.
"Is that bad?"

Hailey coughed, then took a quick drink of water to

cover up her reaction. "Your mommy probably had other things to think about and other things to do."

"My mommy did lots of things." Natasha examined her sandwich as if deciding which part of the rabbit to remove next. She swung her legs, then bit off the tail. "Like reading and sewing and driving and having long naps in the sunshine. I always had to be quiet then."

Dan put his hand on Natasha's arm. "We don't need to talk about Mommy," he said, his voice quiet.

Natasha gave him a puzzled glance. "Miss Deacon said it was good to talk about Mommy."

Dan shot a frown in Hailey's direction. "Did you tell her that?" he asked, a stern note edging his voice.

Once again she felt as if he was questioning her methods. And once again he was doing it in front of Natasha. They needed to have a teacher-parent "chat" about this later on, but in the meantime she needed to deal with this latest situation.

Hailey set her sandwich down, trying to decide how to approach this, reminding herself to be diplomatic.

"It's healthy to verbalize the past," Hailey said, using words Natasha might not understand.

"But that brings up extreme emotions."

Hailey lifted one slender shoulder in a light shrug, knowing Dan referred to the periodic meltdowns his daughter had gone through. "Expressing those emotions is not a negative, considering the timeline of the loss. But more importantly, burying the past is not healthy. These difficulties have a way of manifesting themselves sooner or later and not always in positive interactions," she replied.

As soon as she saw Dan's stricken expression, chills feathered down her spine. She was speaking about Natasha's losing her mother, but she wondered if her comment resurrected thoughts of Austin.

Since Austin's death, she and Dan had never had the chance to talk about him. Their last conversation had been full of pain and anger and the resoluteness of Dan's decision to leave.

Once again the old questions rose up, the second-guessing that haunted her after she walked away from Dan. What if she hadn't forced him? What if she had been more understanding?

She dismissed the questions, pulling her gaze away from Dan, realizing the futility of returning to the past in this situation. At the time she'd made the best decision for herself. She couldn't have predicted what had happened after she'd broken up with Dan.

Maybe Dan was right. Maybe some things were better left in the past. Maybe moving on and forgetting was the practical thing to do.

"As far as verbalizing memories of Lydia are concerned," she continued, determined not to let the current point of discussion on the table be dropped, "I feel strongly that I am correct, based on various psychological studies that I've read on the subject during my time in university." This time she locked eyes with his determined look, playing her education as her final card.

He blinked, then looked over at Natasha. The confused expression on the little girl's face told Hailey that, thankfully, she didn't understand what they were discussing.

"Okay, so how would this work?" Dan asked.

Hailey sensed his wavering in the question and pressed on, still looking at him.

"I would let her determine the direction of the conversation. Allow some fantasy elements, play along a bit, but then steer the topic back to the present."

Dan simply nodded, drumming his fingers on the table.

"And if it never stops?" His comments seemed to challenge her but beneath them Hailey caught a hint of fear.

"I think you will discover that in time, that will ease away. But time and expressing the sorrow are equally important factors."

"We'll need to talk more about this," he said, lowering his voice.

"Are you guys talking about me?" Natasha piped up, her eager gaze flicking from Dan to Hailey.

Dan cleared his throat. "Yes, we are," he said. "And we're talking about your mommy."

Well, that was a bit of progress, Hailey thought. She turned her attention back to Natasha. "Why don't you tell us some of the things your mommy liked to do?" she asked, taking the conversational initiative.

The huge smile spreading across Natasha's face only reinforced what Hailey had been trying to say to Dan. "We would go swimming in the creek," she said, waving the rest of her sandwich. "She liked to splash me. We would go to the ocean and she would dance with me in my princess costume on the beach. Sometimes we would play hide-and-go-seek." Natasha put her sandwich down, leaning forward, her eyes bright as the memories spilled out. "One time we played it in a grocery store. That was so fun. And Mommy bought popcorn for supper and we went on a secret trip with Mommy's friend, Harold, and Daddy was mad because he wasn't invited."

Dan cleared his throat and Hailey couldn't help quickly glancing his way. His lips were pressed together as if stifling his own comments.

While Natasha talked, however, Hailey got a clear picture of what Natasha's life was like with Lydia. Erratic, interesting and nothing like Dan's well-ordered, agenda-driven lifestyle that could drive Hailey crazy sometimes.

More questions bubbled to the surface of her conscious-ness. How had Lydia and Dan met? How had he ended up marrying someone so completely different? Or had that been her appeal?

Then Natasha sighed and her features melted into a sad uncertainty, as if the memories reinforced what she had lost.

She sniffed and a few tears drifted down her cheek, shining in the light cast by the lamp above them. "I miss my mom," she said, her voice hoarse with pain.

Dan shot Hailey a knowing glance, as if Natasha's sad-ness punctuated his previous protests, but Hailey didn't flinch. She knew she was right to encourage Natasha to talk about her mother and that tears were a natural result of bringing up those memories.

Dan drew his daughter into the shelter of his arms, laying his head on hers. Once again Hailey couldn't look away from the obvious love Dan had for his little girl. It created a throb of regret for the relationship she'd never had with her own father.

This little girl does not realize how blessed she is, Hailey thought, getting up to tug a few tissues from the box that Dan's mother always had sitting on the refrig-erator. When she got back Dan was talking to Natasha in low, comforting tones. She wasn't crying anymore, but she stayed ensconced on her father's lap.

Hailey handed Dan the tissues. He wiped Natasha's eyes, then dropped a light kiss on the top of her head. "Are you going to be okay, munchkin?" he asked, his voice low.

She nodded as she drew in a wavering breath. "Can I go get my princess wand? I think it can make me feel happy."

Dan nodded and she slipped off the chair, trudging down the hall.

Sorrow pinched Dan's face as he watched her go. Then,

with another sigh, he pushed himself away from the table, picked up his and Natasha's plates and walked to the kitchen.

Hailey took her own plate and followed him.

"In time, it will get better," she assured him, setting her plate on the counter. "I still believe she needs to articulate what she's dealing with."

"It's hard to watch," Dan said, his voice breaking a little as he leaned back, his hands resting behind him on the edge of the countertop.

Hearing him speak his own pain was hard for her as well. She felt an onslaught of pity for him and had to clench her fists to prevent herself from reaching out and comforting him.

So she stayed where she was, the few feet between them looming as large as Hartley Creek Canyon. They had to keep their lives separate. She had her plans in place and she wasn't wavering from them because an old boyfriend had come back to town.

He's more than an old boyfriend, her conscience accused her.

But she ignored the insidious voice and, as if underlining the distance between them, she took a step away. "I'll wait until you're done for the day before I leave," she said, keeping her voice even and professional.

Dan shook his head. "You're a tutor, not a nanny."

"I know, but you can't have Natasha running around downstairs unsupervised and I don't mind watching her until the store is closed." Hailey was pleased with how reasonable she sounded.

Dan's frown deepened but Hailey knew that, for now, he had few options.

"Okay. Thanks again for helping me out." He waited a

moment, as if he wanted to say more, but then pushed himself away from the counter.

"Before you go," she said, "I need to talk to you about my teaching methods with Natasha."

Dan shot her a resigned look and, crossing his arms, rested his hip against the counter again. "Go ahead."

He didn't sound very encouraging, but Hailey, feeling a bit flush from her previous small victory, pushed on.

"I know you might not agree with my methods and what I'm doing, but I really need to emphasize that I'm a trained teacher. I may not be a psychologist, but I understand how to deal with students who won't fit with the usual pattern of classroom discipline."

My goodness, listen to me, she thought. *I sound like I'm lecturing him.* And from the way he lifted one eyebrow at her, she knew he agreed.

She spread her hands. "All I'm trying to say is, you want me to teach Natasha. Trust me to do it my way."

Dan caught the corner of his lower lip between his teeth. "But really? In the store?"

"I told you I would be discreet and I think it's important for Natasha to know that she can see you from time to time."

"And how will that work when she's back at school?"

"But, you see, we're not putting her back in the school until we know she can make the transition. Make the move," Hailey corrected.

"I know what transition means," Dan said dryly.

"Sorry. I just sounded too much like a teacher."

Dan released a gentle laugh. "I guess I have to keep reminding myself that you are one. A teacher, that is."

"I have new skills. What can I say." She attempted a smile, pleased to see one in return.

He laughed again. "I guess that happens when you don't

see each other for seven years." Then he grew serious. "I still can't believe it's been that long."

His quiet admission hooked like a barb in her heart.

"Well, it has been," she said with a brisk note in her voice, reminding herself of Natasha and Lydia and all the events that had come between them during those seven years. "It's a cliché, but true. Time does march on. Natasha is six years old, after all." She looked directly at him, reminding him of his obligations.

Dan held her gaze then, and it was as if a shutter fell over his features. "That she is." He pushed himself away from the counter. "And as far as working with her in the store is concerned, go ahead. Just keep it reasonable."

Hailey's shoulders lowered. She didn't even realize she'd been holding them up.

"But if I feel like I don't think it's helping her and it's causing a problem..." Dan let the sentence trail off as if he was unsure what he would do when the time came.

"I'll keep things under control," Hailey promised.

Dan gave her an oblique look and, as he walked away, Hailey blew out a long, slow breath.

Round one—Hailey Deacon.

She hoped she wouldn't have to cross swords with him again. It seemed as if every time they faced each other the awkwardness between them grew.

She wasn't sure she could continue to deal with that.

Chapter Five

❧

"So now I want you to divide them up into piles of three and then count them." Hailey brushed her hair back over her shoulder, the overhead lights enhancing its red-gold shine.

Dan leaned against the metal railing dividing the small appliances from the hardware, watching the two of them, Hailey's red head bent over his daughter's darker one.

Natasha's lips were pursed and her forehead wrinkled in concentration as she dutifully rearranged the bolts that Hailey had laid out on the table beside the scale where they weighed items for sale.

Natasha grinned when she was done. "I have four piles."

"So let's write that down," Hailey said, handing Natasha a pencil. "Four plus three is—"

"Seven." Natasha's triumphant look pulled a reluctant smile from Dan.

Dan's initial reluctance to have Hailey and Natasha downstairs was borne out when he caught himself stopping by the back of the store for the fourth time. And it wasn't just Natasha he watched.

When Dan had seen Natasha barreling around that corner the other day, he'd struggled to keep his frustration down. He had assumed Hailey was teaching his daughter structure and balance. Instead Natasha was running around the store wearing fairy wings and carrying one of the many so-called magic wands Lydia had given her.

When Hailey had insisted this was part of her teaching strategy, Dan had had his doubts. But watching them together, his doubts had shifted from worrying about Natasha in the store to worrying about Hailey in the store.

She was a distraction that he wasn't sure he could deal with.

Hailey made Natasha count the bolts again as she dropped them back in the bin, then made her count the bins as they spun the revolving rack around, looking for something else to work with. She spoke softly but Dan didn't miss an underlying firmness to her tone.

"So how is the teaching going?" he heard his mother saying.

Dan glanced back at his mother. She was watching Natasha and Hailey, a bemused expression on her face.

"I think they're just about done. It's lunchtime."

His mother gave him a wry look. "I suppose you're eating upstairs again?"

"Did you have lunch already?" Dan asked, forestalling the impending questions. His mother loved Hailey and she had made no secret that she saw Hailey as a future daughter.

His own feelings for Hailey were confused enough and growing more so every day. He didn't need his mother rooting for his old girlfriend and mixing him up even more.

"I did," his mother said, her expression growing pensive as she watched Hailey and Natasha. "She really has a knack for working with Natasha, doesn't she?" his mother said. "She's one of those natural teachers. She seems to know exactly what Natasha needs."

"And how is Dad feeling today?" he asked, derailing his mother's train of thought before it could pick up too much steam.

"He said he wants to come to the store tomorrow for a few hours," his mother said with a light shrug of her narrow shoulders, thankfully getting the hint.

"Don't let him push too hard. I've got things under control," Dan said.

His mother gave him another quizzical look and unease stirred through him.

"Do you? Really?" The reflective note in her voice wasn't lost on him, but he didn't respond. "You know how glad your father and I are that you and Natasha are home. You really need to be here."

Apprehension trickled down his back at the serious note in her voice and the way her eyes held his, as if trying to say more than her words could convey. He recognized the look and the tone. After Austin's funeral, she would often pull him aside, using the same voice, as she tried to take his emotional temperature.

"And I'm glad to be home." Dan flashed her a smile. "I also appreciate Dad letting me buy into the business," he added, hoping to divert her now as he had tried to divert her then.

"That had always been the plan," she said, her voice growing quieter. "Even before you left Hartley Creek." She folded her arms over her chest. "But that's not what I want to talk about."

"I'm kind of busy right now, Mom." He pushed away from the railing, trying to get away from the sorrow he saw building in her eyes.

But she caught his arm and gave it a gentle tug. "Please don't keep shutting us out."

It was the plaintive note in her voice that stopped him from moving away, but he didn't turn to face her.

"I want you to know that your father and I love you...." She halted, her voice breaking. "But we sense a darkness in you that we can't break through. You know that you can tell us anything."

Dan shook his head even as her words settled in his soul, striking his guilt with deadly accuracy. "There's nothing to tell, Mom." He shot her a tight smile over his shoulder. "The past is over. Done. I've moved on."

"I know we have," his mother said, tightening her grip on his arm, "but I'm not so sure you have. I feel as if there are unhealed wounds you carry yet." She glanced back at Hailey. "And I have a feeling that Hailey is the one who can help you with that. Help you move from that bleak place I know you go to sometimes."

Dan followed the direction of his mother's gaze, the ache in his heart easing a bit as he watched Hailey. As she flicked her hair over her shoulder it seemed to catch the light and beam it onto them like a promise.

"She's good for you. She always was," his mother was saying.

Dan watched the interplay between Hailey and his daughter, the ache in his heart easing a bit as they laughed together. Then he pulled himself to the present.

"I'm not sure I'm good for her," was his cryptic reply.

A short buzz from the front door signaled the entrance of a customer and, thankfully, brought an end to the conversation.

"We'll talk again," his mother said, then strode to the front, her short bob swinging with every step down the crowded aisle of the store. When she came to the end, she turned and gave him a rueful smile, then disappeared.

He clenched his fists, fighting down his confusion. Reality was he'd had his chance with Hailey and he'd blown it. He didn't deserve her in so many ways. Now his focus was Natasha and he had better remind himself of that.

"Daddy, look. I'm adding," Natasha called out.

Dan turned in time to see Natasha come running over, her fairy wings bobbing behind her as she caught his hand. "Come see," she insisted, dragging him around the divider to where she and Hailey had been working. She pointed to the various piles she had created and the papers beneath each pile. "This says four plus three is seven. And this says three plus three is six. And this says six plus one is seven." She pointed out a few other problems, the pleased note in her voice lifting his spirits.

"That's really good, Natasha. You're getting so smart."

Natasha clasped her hands together, squirming with pleasure at his praise. "Miss Deacon says I'm a really fast learner."

"That's great. You'll be back to school in no time."

Natasha shot him a panicked glance and pulled away from him. "No. I can't go to school. I have to stay with Miss Deacon."

"Someday you'll be back in school," he said, unable to keep the gruff tone out of his voice. "Remember, Miss Deacon is only teaching you for a while," he said, keeping his eyes on his daughter. His mother's comments, though well-meant, had only served to resurrect his old shame and guilt.

Natasha looked stricken, then turned to Hailey as if seeking confirmation. "You're going to teach me all the time, aren't you?"

"I'll teach you as long as you need me," Hailey said, being far more diplomatic than he'd been. "Now, let's clean up this stuff and we can go upstairs and I'll get lunch ready." She turned to him. "Are you joining us for lunch?" she asked, her smile soft and gentle.

It hit him like a punch to the stomach.

"Yeah. But just for a bit," he said, his voice stern.

Her puzzled look made him feel like a heel, but he had to stay in control. Keep Hailey at a distance. *She's only around until Natasha goes to school,* he reminded himself. *Come summer, she'll be gone and out of your life.*

So why did that idea create this bleak hollow in his stomach?

"There you go. You got them all right," Hailey said, going over Natasha's work.

Natasha held up the paper. "I know. I'm pretty smart."

"And you're pretty pretty."

Dan's voice behind her raised the small hairs on Hailey's neck, sent a shiver trickling down her spine.

And put her heart into overdrive. She pushed the emotions down, reminding herself to stay professional.

Yet as he came to stand beside Natasha she shot a quick glance his way. Just as he had this morning, he avoided her glance. "Wow, you made a really nice duck," Dan said to his daughter.

"And I made a robot." Natasha pulled up the other connect-the-dots pictures she'd been working on. "That one wasn't hard because it didn't have lots of numbers."

"What else did you do this morning, besides come into the store?" Dan asked, keeping his attention on Natasha, avoiding Hailey's gaze as she set the table.

"Miss Deacon and I did some reading and she said we could do art, but I want to go in the store with her again after lunch."

"You two had some time down there already. Miss

Deacon should keep you up here for the rest of the day," was his brusque reply.

Hailey couldn't stop her eyes from moving to Dan, but as soon as their gazes connected his shifted away. It was as if he had retreated again. But why?

Natasha seemed to pick up on the tension thrumming through the atmosphere and was strangely subdued, her eyes flickering from Dan to Hailey.

To Hailey's surprise, when they were all served Dan took Natasha's hand. "I think we should pray," he said quietly.

"Just like Hailey does," Natasha said in an overly bright voice.

Dan simply nodded. "Yes, just like Hailey does." He bowed his head and prayed a simple prayer. Before she raised her head, Hailey silently added one of her own.

Please, Lord, help me to understand what is happening with Dan.

In spite of her prayer, the unspoken strain between Dan and Hailey continued through lunch. Thankfully, everyone made short work of their meal.

As soon as Natasha was done, she pushed her plate away. "Did I eat enough?" she asked, glancing from Hailey to Dan as if not sure who she should be asking.

"Yes, you did."

"Of course."

Dan and Hailey spoke at once and Hailey felt like smacking herself. Natasha was Dan's daughter, not hers.

"Can I go play in my room with my new princesses that I got from my other gramma?" Natasha asked as pushed her chair back against the table. Lydia's parents had sent a parcel of gifts for Natasha, which Hailey had used to reward the girl for getting her work done this morning.

This time Hailey said nothing, but neither did Dan.

Natasha's confusion showed on her face. "Did I ask something bad?"

"No, honey. You didn't," Dan said finally. "If it's okay with Miss Deacon, you can go play with your dolls for a while."

"Of course you can," Hailey quickly added. "You worked very hard this morning."

Natasha sent them one more puzzled look, then walked down the hallway to her bedroom.

Dan shot to his feet and grabbed his plate, striding to the kitchen with it as if he could hardly wait to leave as well.

Hailey waited a moment, then realized she couldn't stand this anymore. Something had changed and she couldn't identify when or how. She wondered if his seeing her and Natasha in the store this morning had bothered him more than he wanted to admit.

If that was the case, she needed to talk to him. She wasn't letting Dan change her mind about her teaching methods.

She followed him to the kitchen where he was scraping the remainders of his lunch off his plate into the sink.

"Is everything okay?"

"Yeah, of course."

Hailey bit her lip at his abrupt response. "You don't sound like everything is okay. I understood you were okay with Natasha coming down to the store."

"I don't have a huge problem with it. She seems to enjoy working downstairs." Dan rinsed his plate with quick movements, then dropped it and the utensils into the dishwasher.

Hailey's confusion grew. "But you looked angry this morning, when I was finished with Natasha. And just now you said you don't want her downstairs."

"Well, it's just, she needs routine." He washed his hands, then reluctantly turned back to her.

"We talked about this," she said, thoroughly puzzled now. "I feel like we're going in circles. I need to be clear on this. Is it okay if I bring Natasha down to the store or not?"

"My mother isn't comfortable with the idea," was his strange reply.

Hailey's puzzlement shifted to frustration. "That's odd. While I was working with Natasha your mom specifically spoke with me, telling me how happy she was that I was working with Natasha. She said nothing about having a problem with me being down in the store."

Dan looked away and didn't say anything.

"What's going on, Dan? This morning everything seemed fine and now it's like we're back to you not trusting me and my methods."

Dan blew out a sigh and shook his head. "I trust you."

"So what's the problem then?"

He pulled his hands over his face and then looked directly at her. "I don't know what's wrong. Everything. Nothing. I used to know exactly what I wanted, but now..." He finished his sentence with a shrug.

"I'm sure coming back home has been hard for you," Hailey said, folding her arms across her midsection. "It must bring back memories, both good and bad."

As she held his gaze she sensed a shift in the atmosphere. A sense of restlessness. Of half-formed thoughts that neither of them dared speak.

"It has." He blew out his breath, as if deflating, and leaned back against the counter behind him.

And to her surprise, he looked as confused and bewildered as she felt.

"Do you want to talk about it?"

Dan slowly shook his head. "It wouldn't do any good."

Hailey frowned. "What do you mean? If something is bothering you about what I'm doing with Natasha, I want to have it out in the open. That's the only way this is going to work."

He gave her a melancholy smile. "It's not about how you are teaching Natasha. You're dong a great job with her. She's come a long ways since you started working with her and I appreciate that."

Hailey's confusion only increased. "So why is there this tension between us?"

Dan sighed again but this time Hailey waited for him to talk.

Finally he looked up at her. "I think it's that I feel as if so much of the stuff I thought I dealt with is still hanging around."

"Stuff like what?"

"Stuff like you and me. How we used to be a couple." Dan paused, his hazel eyes seeming to pierce hers as her heart skipped a beat. What was he trying to say? Where was he going?

"I promised myself when I came back to Hartley Creek that I would keep my focus on my daughter," he continued. "And I don't need any distractions from that."

His statement plunged into her soul like a shard of ice. The intensity of her hurt surprised her. He saw her as a distraction.

Yet why should it bother her? She didn't want any distractions either. She had the course of her life set out. This stay in Hartley Creek was merely for her grandmother's sake. If she was honest with herself, Dan's presence was a complication for her as well.

"I think the reality is, like you said, we used to be a couple," she said, choosing her words as carefully as a rock climber chooses his precarious handholds. "And that can cause uneasiness that can be a distraction too. But we may as well be adult about it, realize our old relationship was there and move on." She forced a smile as she looked up at him again, disappointed at how his blunt pronouncement had made her heart ache. "I want to be comfortable teaching your daughter without all the tension that seems to follow us."

Dan leaned against the counter behind him, tapping his fingers against the edge. Then he looked over at her again. "You're probably right. It will make things easier if we recognize we had a past and move on. Like you said, we're adults. We were so young then."

"We were," Hailey said, with an airy wave, struggling to sound more offhand than she felt. "My goodness, just high school kids."

"Sort of cliché, isn't it?" Dan said quietly.

Hailey released a light laugh. "A bit. But that's okay. Our lives are not as original as we'd like to think."

A moment of silence followed her statement.

Then Hailey reached for her plate and put it in the dishwasher, hoping he didn't notice her trembling hands. "I'm glad we got that out of the way. Now I can get back to work and you can get back to work and we can be normal around each other." She was pleased at how practical she sounded. How grounded.

How mature.

Dan cleared his throat, then said, "You know, I'm sorry for the way things went after Austin died." His voice was quiet.

His words hovered in the silence between them. This was the first time he'd acknowledged the horrible event that had divided their lives into a before and an after.

Regret and sorrow for what might have been twisted her stomach but she couldn't allow it to stay and take hold.

"I'm sorry too," was her guarded response.

"But, like you said, that's in the past," Dan replied. "We should be able to move on and act normal around each other. We used to be friends."

"Still are, I hope," she said, injecting a falsely hearty tone into her voice.

"Still are." He put his hand on her shoulder. The same kind of casual gesture friends use with each other.

But when he looked at her all her intentions slid away and with them, the intervening years.

Dan's eyes held a shadow of regret but even as their gazes held, something else shifted in his features. A shadow of sorrow flitted across his face and for a moment his hand tightened.

Then he blinked, as if coming back from past to present, and he lowered his hand.

"See you later," he said quietly. Then he turned down the stairs leading to the store, closing the door behind them.

Hailey waited a moment, gathering her own scattered wits even as part of her mind mocked her.

Really? Normal? Around a guy who makes your heart shift into overdrive whenever those hazel eyes connect with yours?

She dismissed the voice. She and Dan could get past this. It would take time before they could treat each other as dispassionately as they would any other person in their lives. She had loved him so much, she thought, her heart aching with the memory. He had been everything to her. Reducing all that to mere friendship wasn't impossible.

But neither was it going to be easy.

* * *

"That soup tasted really good, Hailey. Thanks so much," Dan said, wiping his mouth with the napkin she had laid out.

Hailey flashed him a quick smile and he leaned back in his chair, a surprising feeling of well-being washing over him. For five days in a row he hadn't had to make lunch. For five days he hadn't had to worry about Natasha.

For five days he and Hailey had been able to act surprisingly ordinary around each other. He could do this, he thought. Acknowledge they had been good friends and get through the next few days until Natasha was back in school. Once Hailey left town, he could find a new rhythm for himself and Natasha, a new way of doing things and living their life.

The easing of tension also had much to do with his mother, who had backed off the past few days. She hadn't dropped any of her heavy hints about Hailey, which had only served to bring up his own memories of what he and Hailey had once shared.

"Glad you enjoyed it," Hailey said, getting up and reaching for his bowl.

"Natasha and I will take care of this. You've done enough." He reached out and caught her hand.

Her fingers were cool to the touch. As soft as they ever had been.

She jerked her hand back as a frown pinched her brow. "That's okay. I don't mind," she said.

Dan felt a flicker of dismay at his reaction to her. Hardly the reaction of "just friends."

Only a matter of time, he reminded himself. After all, they had both talked about this weirdness between them and brought it out into the open. It would go away. What they had was in the past and going back served no purpose. It was time they moved on.

"C'mon, Natasha, let's start cleaning up," he said, gathering the plates and bowls.

Natasha jumped up and eagerly helped him carry the dishes to the kitchen.

"Miss Deacon is going to the ranch on Sunday night," she said as she laid the plates on the counter. "She's going to have chocolate cupcakes." Natasha gave him a beatific smile. "I love chocolate cupcakes."

"I do too," Dan said, humoring her as he set the dishes in the dishwasher.

Hailey brought the soup pot to the kitchen and set it on the counter. "There's enough here for supper tonight and tomorrow night if you're really stuck," she said.

"That's great." Dan released a slow smile. "I don't mind soup two nights in a row if I don't have to make it."

"I don't want to have soup two times," Natasha stated, then scooted around him to where Hailey was spooning the leftover soup into a plastic container. "Can I come with you to the ranch on Sunday instead? Can I have supper with you and your friends?"

"Natasha, don't be a beggar," Dan said. "Miss Deacon will want to spend time with her friends by herself."

Dan suspected she was going to a family get-together at her cousin Carter's ranch. He remembered going there from time to time when he and Hailey were dating.

"Actually, I'd like to talk to you about that," Hailey said, snapping a lid on a plastic container. "Natasha, can you go into the dining room and finish up that problem we were working on? When you're done we can go downstairs and do some more word matching."

Natasha glanced from Dan to Hailey, as if trying to puzzle out what they might need to discuss. Then, thankfully, she skipped into the dining room, her ponytail bouncing behind her.

Hailey waited until Natasha was settled at the table, then turned back to Dan. Her actions piqued his curiosity. What could she have to say that she didn't want Natasha to hear?

"Remember Adam from Natasha's class? Emma's boy?" Hailey asked. "When Emma invited me to come for supper she suggested Natasha could come as well."

His gut instinct was to say no. He didn't want to have Natasha gone while he hung around the apartment by himself.

"I thought it would be a good opportunity for Natasha and Adam to spend some time together," Hailey continued. "It could help Natasha's transition to the classroom."

Dan glanced through the doorway to the dining room. Natasha appeared engrossed in her work and was not paying attention to them. Nonetheless, he drew a bit closer to Hailey and lowered his voice. "Is he the boy who talked about her crying all the time?" Dan wasn't sure he wanted his daughter spending time with a kid who didn't seem to like her.

"He said that because he was worried about her, that's all."

He looked down at Hailey, her face barely a foot from his. Her gray eyes, her pale skin, all framed by a riot of red hair, sent a surprising flash of attraction through him.

A familiar attraction.

Dan's fingers rasped against his whiskers as he considered the idea. "I've spent enough time sitting by myself over the weekends. I'm not sure I want her away so soon."

Hailey looked away, breaking the connection between them. "Okay. Then why don't you come along?"

This caught him by surprise. He paused, trying the idea on for size. While he would have preferred to have his daughter at home with him, he wasn't sure he wanted to take this opportunity away from her either.

"I suppose I could," he said. "But are you sure it would be okay with your cousin?"

"Future cousin," Hailey corrected. "But yes, I am. It's just dinner. Emma and Carter would love to have you."

"Okay. Then I'll come. Besides, I wouldn't mind catching up with Carter some more. Find out how that drill has been working out for him."

Hailey tugged her sweater over her hands, wrapping her arms around her middle. "Okay, then, I'll phone Emma and tell her you're coming." The hesitancy in her voice resurrected his doubts.

It would be fine, he reasoned. Carter wasn't just Hailey's cousin. He had also, at one time, been a friend.

It would be like old times.

Which could, potentially, be a problem.

Chapter Six

"I am excited to go to a ranch. Have you ever been to a ranch, Daddy?" Natasha bounced on the seat of Dan's truck, her excitement easing away Hailey's concerns about having asked them both along to Carter and Emma's place.

When Dan had agreed to come as well, Hailey had been surprised. Her offer to him had been a courtesy. She hadn't thought he would take her up on it.

She had arrived at church late this morning because she'd had to walk, and had caught only a glimpse of Dan and Natasha as she left. They'd been occupied talking to an older couple and hadn't seen Hailey so she hadn't had a chance to go over their plans.

When Dan called after church to double-check the time, her relief that the trip was still on was frustrating. She guessed the "normal" she wanted to achieve with Dan would take time yet.

"I've been to this ranch," Dan said as he turned the truck onto the road heading out of Hartley Creek toward the Rocking K. "I even rode a horse there!"

"If you want to call that riding," Hailey couldn't help adding, trying to keep things light. Just a couple of old friends reminiscing.

"Only got bucked off once," Dan said.

"You got bucked off a horse?" Natasha was all ears. "Why?"

"Because your daddy forgot to tighten the cinch like someone told him to," Hailey said, her smile widening at the memory. She could still see Dan sailing through the air and flattening the undergrowth when he landed.

"Someone wasn't very specific in her instructions," Dan added, giving her a knowing look.

"Or someone wasn't listening."

"Maybe someone wasn't."

Hailey held his laughing gaze, then turned to watch the snow-covered fields edging the road. Beyond the fields the frozen river snaked along like a silver thread unspooling from the mountains, rising up to cradle the valley. The sun hovered above the mountains, burnishing the hills with a golden color.

A quick glance in the rearview mirror showed her the ski hill overlooking the town, the lights from the lifts starting to appear in the late-afternoon light. Early this morning she'd heard the muted thump of avalanche bombs going off on the hill, which meant the powder on the upper runs would be epic. So she had hitched a ride with Megan to the hill and taken a few runs.

While they were skiing, Megan had mentioned to Hailey that the grade one class would be going every afternoon to the ski hill for lessons. She had said it would be a good opportunity for Natasha to spend time with her future classmates in a more casual setting.

Though Megan had encouraged Hailey to talk to Dan about it, Hailey was hesitant to mention the skiing lessons. She wasn't sure how Dan would react to his daughter going skiing on Misty Ridge.

"Do you think I can ride a horse when we are at the ranch?" Natasha was asking.

Hailey turned her attention back to the little girl. "It's a bit cold for riding, but maybe next time you can."

"That would be so fun," Natasha said. "Then I can tell my mommy that I rode—" Her voice broke abruptly and she looked down, fiddling with the pom-poms on the end of her scarf.

Hailey's heart broke for the little girl but to her surprise, no tears came. Natasha simply heaved out a heavy sigh, then said with a plaintive voice, "I don't think I can tell my mommy, can I?"

Hailey slid her arm over the girl's shoulders to comfort her. Dan had the same idea, however, and for a moment both of them held Natasha, their arms overlapping. But neither of them flinched and neither of them pulled back.

Hailey couldn't help another glance over at Dan, pleased with this new shift between them.

It was as if getting away from the store and getting out into the countryside had eased away the disquiet that surrounded him.

She welcomed the change because it made her more relaxed as well.

"I like your pretty necklace," Natasha was saying, eyeing the gold chain Hailey was unconsciously fingering.

Hailey held it up, smiling. "Thank you. I got this from my Nana," she said.

"Is it special?" Natasha asked.

"Very special. It came from a bracelet my Nana had. The bracelet had five gold nuggets that came from my great-great-grandmother. Her name was Kamiskahk."

"That's a funny name," Natasha said.

"It's a Kootenai name," Dan added. "You should tell Natasha the story. It's very interesting."

Hailey shot Dan a surprised look, then remembered that he knew the story of Kamiskahk as well. Her Nana had told him when Dan had asked her about the bracelet that she always wore.

Another link between them.

"Can you tell me the story?" Natasha asked.

"Kamiskahk's father hadn't told anyone else in the tribe about the gold nuggets and he told his daughter to keep them a secret when he gave them to her. Then my great-great-grandfather, August Beck, came to the valley. He met Kamiskahk and fell in love."

"Did he get hurt?" Natasha asked, her eyes wide.

"Maybe a bit," Hailey said with a laugh. When she looked at Dan it was to discover him looking at her. She forced herself to hold his gaze then gave him a quick smile, pleased to see him return it.

See? They could do normal.

"Anyway, August found out about the nuggets," Hailey continued. "And he got gold fever."

"I got fever once," Natasha put in. "My mommy said it would go away, but it didn't. I had to go to the hospital."

Another glimpse of the little girl's life with her mother. Which made Hailey wonder, yet again, what kind of woman Lydia had been. And what had Dan seen in her?

That was none of her business. That was Dan's life and Dan's past and she had no right to that. Not anymore.

"Well, gold fever isn't really like being sick. It means he wanted to find gold very badly and he'd do almost anything for it," Hailey said, carrying on with her story. "So August left the village and went looking for the gold. He spent weeks and months but couldn't find any. Then one day he felt cold and tired and he started thinking about Kamiskahk. And he realized he had made a mistake but he was too ashamed to go back and admit it."

"Did he ever go back?" Natasha asked, leaning closer and touching the gold nugget at the end of the necklace.

"Yes, he finally did make the right choice. And he and Kamiskahk got married and they had a boy named Able, who had a boy named Bill, who married my Nana Beck. And the gold nuggets were passed down and my grandpa Bill made them into a bracelet for my Nana. And my Nana then got a necklace made out of each nugget and she gave them to her five grandchildren. And I'm one of the grandchildren."

Natasha nodded, her attention riveted on the necklace.

"I always liked that story," Dan said, slowing down to make the final turn to the ranch. "I'm just curious, what made your Nana decide to break the bracelet apart? I know she treasured it."

Hailey twined the chain around her finger, thinking of the evening her Nana had given it to her, along with the Bible. How Nana had hoped she would take the story seriously and be encouraged to make the right choices in her life, just as August had.

"I guess she wasn't sure about giving it to either of her daughters. Carter and Garret's mom died when the boys were little and I know she and my mom weren't close. I guess she decided to skip a generation. And it worked out pretty good. Five kids, five nuggets."

"That's a great legacy," Dan said, looking at her across the cab. "You're lucky to have it."

As Hailey held his gaze, other parts of her legacy came to mind. How her father had left her and her sisters. How her mother had moved away, leaving Hailey, seemingly without a second thought.

How Dan had also left her.

Hailey pulled her gaze away. "Yes. I am. But I'm also

very thankful that my Nana gave it to me. I'm thankful we still have her with us."

"Will she be here tonight?" Dan asked.

"Oh yes. Wherever two or more grandchildren are gathered, Nana is there."

Dan looked like he was about to say more but then Natasha leaned forward, straining against her seat belt, pointing. "Is that it? Is that the ranch?"

They had rounded a corner and were approaching a group of buildings. The snow crunched beneath their tires as they slowed down.

The barns and corrals lay to one side of the large yard. On the other were two houses, one smaller than the other. Smoke poured out of the chimneys of both houses, and lights shone from the windows with a welcoming glow. A few cars were parked in front of the larger house, where Emma and Adam lived.

"What are those little houses?" Natasha asked, pointing to the three structures beyond the large red barn and the corrals.

"Those are cabins," Hailey said as Dan parked beside Shannon's little car. When Shannon had found out Hailey was coming, she'd offered her a ride. When Hailey had told her sister she would be riding with Dan and Natasha, she'd endured a long, meaningful pause more expressive than anything Shannon could have said. Hailey hoped her sister would keep her negative comments to herself tonight. Shannon had made no secret of the fact that she thought Hailey was playing with fire, spending so much time with Dan.

"Who lives there?" Natasha asked, yanking at her seat belt.

"Carter lives in one of them," Hailey said, helping her unbuckle the belt. "But before that, me and my sisters would stay in them whenever we came to visit our Nana, Grandpa, and Garret and Carter. They all lived in the big house, the one we're going to right now."

"Can we go to the cabins? Can we see inside?" Natasha asked, tugging on her toque and mitts, as if fully expecting to go look at them right away.

"We first have to go to the house. But maybe later I can show you my old cabin." Hailey stepped out of the truck into the chilly air. As she did, wistfulness plucked her heart. She'd visited the ranch a couple of times since she'd been back, of course, but each time a new set of memories surfaced. The games she and her cousins played, the hikes they made, the hot dog roasts and the horseback trips.

And this time, memories of the few visits she and Dan had made here assaulted her. She choked those thoughts down. They belonged in the past.

Smoke wafted out of the nearest cabin, and a weak light shone from its window. After Emma and Carter got engaged, she'd moved to the big house and Carter had moved into the cabin Emma had been staying in when she was simply a hired hand on the ranch.

So much had changed for Carter, she thought, hugging herself. Once he'd been so broken, but Emma and her boy had healed him.

She forced herself not to look at Natasha or Dan. Theirs was a different story, she reminded herself. She and Dan had had their chance. Too many events were crowded between then and now.

Besides, she had her own plans.

An undisturbed blanket of snow covered Naomi's cabin. No one had visited it since winter had come. While she looked at the cabin, Hailey sent up a prayer for her sister keeping watch over her dying fiancé.

Beside Naomi's was Hailey's cabin. The path leading

up to it still held the vague shapes of her footprints from the last time she'd been here. She had shoveled the snow off the veranda then and had sat there for a while, letting herself get drawn into the innocence of the past. The simplicity of her life at that time.

Natasha tugged on her hand, pulling her out of her reverie. "Let's go to the house and ask Mr. Beck if I can ride a horse."

Hailey was about to reply when Dan came around the front of the truck and knelt down in the snow in front of her. "We're not asking Mr. Beck anything," he said, catching her by the shoulders and turning her to him as he established some ground rules for his daughter. "That's rude, okay?"

Natasha glanced up at Hailey as if to ask her to advocate for her.

"We're here to visit," Hailey said. "So I think your daddy is right."

Natasha pushed her lip out in a pout. "I mean it, Natasha," Dan reiterated. "No asking."

Natasha sighed, then nodded as she took Hailey's hand, then Dan's. Together they led her to the house, the snow squeaking under their feet as they walked. Hailey tried not to look over at Dan and the little domestic scene they had created, the two of them walking with Natasha between them.

The door of the house swung opened as soon as they stepped onto the veranda. Emma stood framed in the doorway, the light behind her burnishing her dark hair. She wore a loose sweater over blue jeans and bare feet, in spite of the cold. "Come in, come in," Emma called out, waving them into the house.

Hailey pulled Natasha along behind her and as they entered the house warmth washed over them, laced with the mouthwatering smells of supper cooking. Laughter bursting from the living room beyond the kitchen added to the cozy ambience.

"Carter, Shannon and Nana are trying to play a new game Shannon bought at a garage sale," Emma explained as she took Dan and Natasha's coats and hung them up in a closet in the porch. "Go inside, Dan. Make yourself at home. Natasha, Adam has been waiting for you. He's in the living room setting up the farm set."

Dan nodded, then walked into the kitchen, Natasha right on his heels. Hailey went to follow when Emma caught her by the arm, pulling her back.

"So?" Emma asked, the single word dripping with innuendo. She tucked a strand of her long, dark hair behind an ear, her brown eyes brimming with curiosity. Emma had been around the family long enough to know Hailey's history, romantic and otherwise, and was obviously curious about Dan's presence here.

Hailey held her eager gaze, then said, "How are the wedding plans coming?"

Emma tilted her head to one side, hoop earrings flashing in the light of the porch, then she grinned. "I just find it interesting that Dan came along," she said, ignoring Hailey's attempt to head her off at the conversational impasse.

Hailey's only answer was to crane her neck to see where Dan was, making sure he couldn't hear her. Then she turned back to her future cousin-in-law and lowered her voice. "This is the deal. I'm only telling you once. Dan is very protective of his daughter and he didn't want her coming along by herself. That's it. That's the whole reason and the only reason he's here." She underlined this with a slice of her hand. "Yes, we used to date. Yes, we used to be serious. But I broke up with him and now he's a widower with a little girl. What we had is beyond ancient history. The Mesopotamians are modern compared to what me and Dan had. Okay?"

Emma pursed her lips and folded her hands as she considered Hailey. Then she sighed in resignation. "Okay. I get it."

"Thanks." At least that was settled.

"But I still think there's something going on."

Hailey simply rolled her eyes, spun around and strode into the house. Seriously! Family!

"I imagine you're happy with the cattle prices right now," Dan said to Carter as he leaned back against the couch.

Dinner was over and under orders from the women, he and Carter had been sent to the living room while they cleaned up the dishes and made tea and coffee. A fire crackled in the large stone fireplace, sending out welcome waves of warmth.

"Not complaining," Carter agreed, lounging back in his recliner, his wavy hair a dark contrast against the beige upholstery. "It's helped us turn a favorable corner."

"And it's meant Carter can afford to keep me in the manner to which I'm accustomed," Emma said, setting out a tray of teacups and coffee mugs on the low table in the living room.

"What manner is that?" Hailey asked with a laugh as she spooned some sugar into a teacup and handed it to Nana.

"Oh, you know, barefoot, in the kitchen," Emma said with a wink toward Carter.

"I hope the third part of that very rude statement will come true someday," Nana said, stirring her tea, her graying hair setting off her slate-blue eyes.

"One thing at a time, Nana," Emma said, holding out a mug for Dan. "Coffee?"

"Sounds good." He took it and Emma held out the sugar bowl.

"He only takes cream," Hailey said handing him the pitcher.

He felt an instant of surprise that she remembered.

"And how are wedding plans coming?" Shannon asked Emma. "Will Garret be back in time to stand up for you, Carter?"

"He better be," Carter growled. "He said the job in Dubai would be done by then."

"I'm sure he'll be back," Hailey said. "Garret always does what he promises."

"Used to, anyway," Carter said, looking down at his coffee.

No one responded to that enigmatic comment and the women were drawn into wedding talk. Dan was content to sit back and watch the interaction.

All during dinner the conversations would bypass each other, interweave, join up and double back. Sentences would be started by one, finished by another. A single word would elicit peals of laughter.

Emma and Dan would look at each other and shrug.

Dan couldn't help a tinge of envy at Hailey's connection with her cousins. His parents had moved to Hartley Creek as a young couple, leaving family behind in Houston, Texas, and Windsor, Ontario. Because the store kept his parents busy six days a week and most weeks of the year, they didn't often get away to visit extended family.

So for the majority of his life it had been just him and Austin.

And now it was just him and Natasha.

He took a quick sip of coffee, then coughed. Too hot.

"You okay?" Hailey asked, throwing him a questioning look.

"Fine. Just fine." He held his hand up to assure her.

"And how is your father doing, Dan?" Nana was asking. "Is he recuperating?"

"He's doing okay. Still gets tired quickly," Dan said. "The doctor said he's never seen such a bad case of pneumonia, but he's getting stronger every day."

"I know your parents are very glad to have you back," Nana said, glancing around her own brood. "We do miss our children after a while. And I know your parents were never the same after your brother died on the ski hill."

"No. I guess they weren't," Dan muttered, cradling his coffee mug in his hands, her innocent comment agitating a storm of old feelings.

"I know how hard it was for me to bury my daughter Noelle, Carter and Garret's mother. I'm sure your parents felt the same." Nana Beck lifted her hand in a gesture of helplessness. "It was difficult to see your parents deal with all their grief. They became shadows of their former selves."

"Daddy, come and see what me and Adam did," Natasha called out. "We're making a farm."

Dan put his mug down so fast the contents sloshed around, almost spilling. "I should...I should go see what's she's been doing," Dan said, seizing the opportunity to leave an increasingly uncomfortable conversation.

"Of course. Of course," Nana said, waving him off. "I'm so sorry if what I said hurt you. I didn't mean anything."

"No, it's fine." Dan moved to where his daughter sat. As he crouched down beside her on the carpet, the heat from the fireplace warmed a chill that had gripped him. "So, what are you kids doing here?"

"See, we've got all the goats together because Adam

said that's how it's supposed to be," Natasha said, pointing to a plastic pen. "And over here are the chickens. They have to be close to the barn so they can go inside quick if a coyote comes."

"Or a fox," Adam intoned as he moved a few sheep around.

"I never seen a fox," Natasha said.

"They are bad for chickens."

Dan let their chatter wash over him. He felt a bit rude for leaving Nana so quickly, but her comments about his parents cut him deep and hard. Her words had ignited the guilt that seemed to be his constant companion since he'd seen that covered sled coming off the ski hill, holding his brother's body.

He hooked the tractor to a baler for Adam, then helped Natasha move the barn. After a few moments he glanced over at the adults and caught Hailey looking at him.

Her wistful smile made his heartbeat tick upward and when she got up to join them, his emotions tipped into anticipation.

"This looks amazing," Hailey said, standing over them.

"My daddy is a good farmer," Natasha replied, intent on the fence she was assembling for the horses.

"I'm sure he is," Hailey said. But she didn't sit down with them. "I just thought I'd let you know, I'm heading over to my cabin to pick up a few things. And anytime you want to go, Dan, is fine with me."

Natasha's head spun around at that. "Can I come? Can I see the cabin?" She clambered to her feet.

Dan caught his daughter by the arm. "No, honey. I think Miss Deacon wants to go by herself."

Natasha's lower lip started moving out and she sent a pleading look Hailey's way.

But Dan wasn't giving in to her. Not in front of Hailey's family. Besides, it was time his daughter heard the word *no*.

Hailey sent Dan a look that clearly telegraphed it was okay with her, but Dan shook his head. "Natasha can stay here. You go." He glanced at his watch. "I wouldn't mind to be back in town soon. I need to stop in at my parents' place as well." He hadn't seen his father since day before yesterday and wanted to let him know how things were going at the store.

"Okay, if I'm not back in time, come and get me." And then Hailey turned and left.

Dan wasn't going to watch her, but he couldn't keep his eyes off her slim figure, moving with an easy grace, her hair a copper fall, swinging with every step.

"Daddy, why are you staring at Miss Deacon?" Natasha asked.

Dan quickly averted his gaze, hoping the rest of Hailey's family hadn't heard what she'd said.

But more than that, hoping Hailey hadn't heard what she'd said.

Stay focused, he reminded himself as he tried to keep his attention on what his daughter was doing. *You can't afford to get distracted.*

And yet, even as he told himself this, he couldn't erase the picture of Hailey from his mind.

Chapter Seven

Hailey shivered in the chill of the cabin and turned up the temperature on the little heater, wondering why she bothered. By the time the cabin was warm it would be time to go.

But at least for now, it took some of the bite off the cold air.

She glanced around the cabin, memories crowding each other. She'd had so many good times here.

She got on her knees and reached under the bed, ignoring the rolling dust bunnies as she pulled out a shoe box. She set it on the bed and brushed the dust off.

Pain stabbed through her when she saw the writing on the lid.

Letters and notes from Dan, with a date scribbled beneath the title.

She knew she should toss the box aside to be discarded. But in spite of herself she rested her hand on the box, her lips pressed together as memories assaulted her.

When she'd made the decision to move away from Hartley Creek, she'd thrown away what she could and moved the rest to her cabin here. It wasn't much. A few boxes of photos, some CDs, some books and memorabilia. A couple of old snowboards that, at one time, she had scrimped and saved for and hadn't been able to part with, even after she'd broken them.

And in the box below her hand, some of the notes she and Dan had sent each other throughout high school and after he'd graduated.

The date scribbled on the lid was four days before Austin's accident. A month before Dan left Hartley Creek.

With a decisive movement, she set the box aside, then went under the bed again and found the box she'd come looking for. This one held some old CDs she wanted to hear again. A few movies she could watch again. Stuff. She set it aside, found another box that held books and set them both by the door. Hopefully, Dan wouldn't mind putting them in the back of the truck. She glanced around the cabin. In a few months she would be moving again and anything she left behind would be here for a long time.

She was about to go, but her eyes shifted to the box on the bed. She had to find a way to get rid of it. Maybe Carter could burn the letters.

What if he looked through them?

She snatched the box off the bed and quickly brought it to the pile by the door. This she had to do herself. But if she was taking them back to Hartley Creek in Dan's truck she'd have to bag the box up, or find a way to seal it shut so the lid wouldn't come off in transport. Maybe Emma had something in the house she could use.

Before she left, however, she walked back to the corner where her old snowboards stood. Bright red and orange flames decorated one of them.

She picked it up, grinning at the huge crack between the two bindings on the board, remembering how it had happened. She and Megan had just carved through some awesome powder and ended up on the edge of a double black diamond, squinting against the sun dancing off a thick layer of snow that had fallen the night before. Below them lay the town of Hartley Creek, bisected by the river. Dan had taken his brother Austin down an easier run and was waiting for them at the bottom of the hill. Hailey knew if she didn't get down soon, Dan would be up the chairlift again and she would have a hard time finding him. So she'd taken Megan's dare.

Halfway down she hit some exposed rock, tumbled, turned over, hit another rock with her board and that was the end of snowboarding that day. When she'd finally caught up with Dan he'd been furious. That was when Hailey knew he really cared for her.

They'd started going steady after that.

Hailey was about to set the board back against the wall when a knock on the door startled her. She jumped around, dropping the snowboard with a clatter.

"Can I come in?" Dan called out.

Hailey was surprised by the tremor in her chest at the sound of his deep voice. She smoothed her hair away from her face, then caught herself preening. With a shake of her head she walked to the door and opened it.

To her surprise he stood by himself on the deck, shadows flickering over his face from the single bulb hanging from the ceiling behind Hailey.

"Where's Natasha?" she asked as he stepped into the cabin.

"She got distracted by a video game she and Adam are playing." Dan looked past her and grinned. "Are those your old snowboards?" he asked.

"I should throw them away, but haven't been able to." Hailey shoved her hands in the back pocket of her blue jeans, suddenly far too aware of how small the cabin had become when Dan had come inside.

Why had he come?

Probably just to hurry her along. He had said he wanted to leave early.

But he picked up the board she had set aside, seemingly not in any rush to go yet. "I remember this one. Didn't you name it Red Lightning?"

Hailey shrugged, surprised he remembered and a little embarrassed at the same time. "I know. Not exactly original or accurate."

"I remember how the sales guy at Edge of the Sky laughed at you when you christened it with that bottle of water."

"Was a big day for me," Hailey answered, letting his easy comments pull her back into the drift of old memories. "My first brand-new snowboard, and a Burton to boot. I can't remember how many kids I babysat or how many dishes I washed at the Royal to pay for it."

"Lots, I'm sure. Boards are expensive." Dan picked it up, his long fingers tracing the crack running across the bottom. He grinned as he set it aside. "You were a bit of a daredevil on the hill. I remember how hard I had to push myself to keep up with you." His smile was relaxed, easy, and as their eyes met it was as if the events and relationships of the past few years shifted to the side and they were simply Dan and Hailey again.

Silence hovered between them but this time it was the quiet comfort of old friends. Which is what they were.

Hailey had known Dan since she had moved to Hartley Creek. Though he was a year older, in a small town that didn't matter as much, and they'd grown up together.

"I'm glad Natasha is enjoying playing with Adam," Hailey said, pushing the snowboard Dan had just set down into the corner again. "That will make her transition into school easier."

"That's good for her. Natasha hadn't had much chance to play with other kids when she lived with Lydia. Or, for that matter, when she came to visit me."

Hailey pulled in one corner of her lip. "Did Lydia really do any homeschooling with Natasha?"

Dan shook his head, releasing a bitter laugh. "I think you've seen the results of that. Lydia had all these grand ideas, but she wasn't good on the follow-up."

Hailey pulled her coat around her, surprised that Dan had been the one to bring up his ex-wife. Other than the brief mention of Lydia's parents, it was as if they had an unspoken agreement not to talk about her.

But Hailey's curiosity was piqued, especially hearing Dan's tone when he spoke of her.

"Your divorce must have been difficult for you as well as Natasha."

Dan gave her a wry look. "Actually, this sounds a bit harsh, but it was a bit of a relief."

This was news to Hailey. "Why?"

Dan scratched his temple with one finger and eased out a sigh. Then, to her surprise, he sat down on the stool behind him. Hailey took the hint and lowered herself to the bed, waiting.

"Lydia and I didn't have the best marriage. It started for the wrong reasons." He wove his fingers together, tapping his thumbs against each other, the grimness of his features throwing his eyes into shadow. He said nothing for a moment and Hailey had to stifle the questions bubbling beneath the surface. "You may as well know…Lydia and I…" He paused, his attention on his hands, avoiding her gaze. "When I left Hartley Creek I felt depressed. I didn't live the life I should have." He lifted his shoulder in a shrug. "There's no excuse for it, but I hung out with a bad crowd. Partied too much. Made some dumb mistakes."

Hailey pressed her lips together, sensing they were edging toward unknown territory. Moving toward a place from which, once entered, there would be no turning back.

A frisson of fear trickled down her spine. Did she want to go there? Would it change things between her and Dan?

Right now she had her life mapped out. And, apparently, Dan had his own goals too. And neither figured in the other's future plans.

And yet, all those questions she had agonized over when she found out about Lydia still hovered at the edges of her consciousness. Maybe, if they could be answered, it would ease some of the lingering brokenness that she had carried all this time, even make it easier for her to leave when the time came.

"What happened, Dan?" Hailey slipped the question into the quiet following his initial admission.

He said nothing at first and even the shadows behind them seemed to hold their breath, waiting.

Dan squeezed his hands together. "Like I said, I made some bad decisions. Some big mistakes. I was lonely and still trying to deal with all the…all the stuff that happened back here." He stopped, then looked up at Hailey. "Lydia and I ended up together one night. She got pregnant. I knew I had to step up to my responsibilities, so I told her we had to get married. And we did. Then, two years after Natasha was born, Lydia left me and filed for divorce."

As he spoke, it was as if something deep within her was torn up by the roots. All her old thoughts, bitterness and sorrow had been grounded in wrong perceptions. False conclusions.

"That's why you married her? Because of Natasha?" She had to say it again, to hear the confirmation from him.

Dan nodded, looking down at his hands, his mouth set in angry lines. "Yes. That's why. It wasn't because I loved

Lydia. It was because I wanted to do what was right. To fix my mistakes."

As Hailey's breath left her lungs, she became aware she'd been holding it.

"I'm not sorry I did that," Dan added. "I knew I had to man up to my responsibilities. My regret is for the mistakes I made that required me to marry her."

Regret. He felt regret for mistakes.

Hailey rocked back and forth; Dan's admission had created a seismic shift reverberating backward through her memories and through her life.

He hadn't married Lydia because he loved her.

Which made Hailey wonder how Dan had felt about her when he'd left.

Dan's eyes were full of sorrow and pain as his gaze caught hers. "I'm sorry you had to hear this, Hailey. I'm not proud of what I did."

"But you did the right thing," Hailey said, pressing her hands to her heated cheeks. "You absolutely did the right thing. And now you have Natasha and I'm sure you don't regret that."

Dan's grateful smile dove into her heart and settled there.

"No. I don't," he said quietly. "I guess God hadn't given up on me. He found a way to make her a blessing to me."

The only sound in the ensuing silence was the hum of the heater. The cabin walls isolated them from the rest of the world, creating a momentary haven.

Outside lay responsibilities and decisions. But right here and right now it was just the two of them dealing with the brokenness that had come between them.

"I'm glad you told me about Lydia," Hailey said, rubbing her hands up and down her denim-clad legs. "Really glad."

Dan blew out a long, slow sigh. "Not easy to admit the stupid mistakes a person does, but I knew if we ever met again I'd have to tell you. Especially because at one time we were close."

At one time. The words had a finality to them that created a pang of wistfulness.

"Yes, we were," Hailey said, getting to her feet, looking over at the snowboard, then at the boxes beside the door. "And now we should probably get back to the house before people think you got lost."

Or before they think something else.

Dan stood at the same time and then they were inches apart. Hailey swallowed, her mind telling her to move but her heart wanting this moment of closeness.

"Hailey, I'm so sorry," Dan whispered. Then he lifted his hand and rested it on her shoulder. Squeezed ever so slightly.

Even through her jacket she felt his warmth. Then, without thinking why, she lifted her shoulder, and pressed her cheek against his hand.

Dan's hand squeezed tighter, and then his other hand moved to her other shoulder, pulling her closer. Her hand lifted and rested on his chest, her fingers curling against the rough material of his wool jacket.

She moved nearer.

Emotions old and new roiled around them, pulling, pushing, woven through with a sense of waiting. Anticipation.

A sharp rap on the door splintered the moment.

Hailey jumped back, her cheeks flaming. Dan lowered his hand and moved away.

"Come in," Hailey called out, shoving her hands in her pocket as she strode toward the door.

Emma put her face inside, glancing from Hailey to Dan.

"Natasha was wondering where Dan had gone. She wants to show him something on the computer."

"Of course," Hailey said, clenching her hands inside her pockets. "We'll be right there. Dan was helping me figure out which boxes I can put in the truck. I guess it's okay if I leave the snowboards here unless they're in the way?" She heard the nervousness in her voice. *Way to sound guilty,* she chided herself.

The glint of humor in Emma's brown eyes told Hailey she thought the same thing.

"There's no rush. I just wanted to make sure Dan found the right cabin and wasn't wandering around the yard."

Then, with a discreet wink to Hailey, Emma closed the door, leaving Dan and Hailey behind.

"We should probably head back to town," Dan said, looking everywhere but at Hailey. "I promised my parents I'd stop in tonight with Natasha."

"Of course. I'll get these boxes to the truck and see you at the house." Hailey didn't look at Dan as he closed the door behind himself but she was sure he saw her flushed cheeks.

Stupid fair complexion, she thought, gathering up the boxes. Dead giveaway every time.

Dead giveaway of what? He's not supposed to mean anything to you anymore.

Hailey shook her head as if to dislodge the accusing voice. He didn't. That moment with Dan had been born of an intimate conversation. It was an aberration.

So why did Hailey feel as if they were on the edge of something else?

Chapter Eight

"No. I don't want her going on the ski hill." Dan knelt on the floor and ripped open the box of drill bits he had brought up from the back room.

It was a Monday morning. The lunch rush was over and his mother was taking care of the lone customer in the store.

Which was probably why Hailey sprung this on him now.

"It will be a good opportunity for her to connect with the other kids." Hailey stood beside him and from the corner of her eye he saw her pursed lips, her head tipped to one side as if she was trying to figure him out.

Not that he blamed her. Lately he couldn't figure himself out either. One moment he was telling himself that he and Hailey had moved on. That they were mature adults who could interact like any other mature adults.

The next he was almost kissing her in her old cabin at the ranch.

"She can do that when she's back in school," Dan retorted, pulling out a couple of blister packages.

"We talked about transition," Hailey said. "I think this

could be another good step for her to integrate back into the class in a nonthreatening environment."

"I'd hardly call Misty Ridge a nonthreatening environment." As Dan stood, he couldn't stop a thrum of anxiety at the thought of his daughter on the ski hill. "She's too young yet," he said, looking over Hailey's shoulder. Natasha was working in the back of the store again, sorting some nuts and bolts. Dan couldn't figure out why she seemed to enjoy that so much, but Hailey was able to show results by doing it. And he wasn't going to argue with results.

But he was going to argue with Hailey's proposition. He turned his attention back to her. "She's never been on the ski hill, or any ski hill for that matter."

"The younger she can start the better it will be for her." Hailey sounded reasonable, but he couldn't get his emotions past the thought of his daughter skiing on Misty Ridge.

"Better for what?" he said, turning back to sorting the drill bits. Why had Hailey sprung this on him while he was working and distracted? Had she hoped he would simply agree and leave it at that?

"It would be better for her confidence and for her skills."

"She doesn't need to learn how to ski or snowboard." As Dan hung the blister pack of three-eighths-inch bits on the peg he realized how silly he sounded.

"Considering that the ski hill is a scant ten-minute drive from town, I would think sooner or later she'll end up on Misty Ridge," Hailey said. "May as well equip her with the skills she needs as early as possible."

As much as he hated the idea, Dan also knew she was right. And he also knew that in a town like Hartley Creek, where skiing and snowboarding were imbedded in the culture of the town, it was inevitable Natasha would get drawn into it.

"I still don't like it," he insisted.

"She had so much fun with Adam at the ranch," Hailey said, pressing on as if she sensed his wavering. "This would be a logical next step. Besides, like I said, it is a nonthreatening situation for her and for her classmates."

"You know I don't like the idea and I'm sure you know why," he finally admitted.

"Of course I know why," she said. "I was there that day too, remember?"

He looked over at her and as his gaze held her gray-blue eyes it was as if he had shifted back in time and they were back up on the mountain. She was leading the way in her usual kamikaze style, daring him to follow her down that double black diamond run. Daring him to follow her into the roped-off areas that held a whiff of danger. He felt the same tickle in the pit of his stomach he experienced when he stood on the edge of a difficult slope. A sense of expectation and exhilaration.

But mixed in with that, a sense of fear.

Because he also remembered her reaction when they'd gotten the news about Austin's death. How she had stumbled backward. Fallen down and then started weeping inconsolably. She had suffered almost as huge a loss as he had. Her grief had been almost as deep as his.

And he had to carry that with him as well.

Hailey took a step closer, laying her hand on his arm. "How about I take her on Monday, just for the day? Now that your dad is better, you can come out and see for yourself how things go with her."

Her hand felt warm and soft, and as he looked down at her face he caught again the orange scent of her perfume. She stood so close that he could see the faint scar along her cheekbone, and before he could stop himself he'd reached up and touched it.

"Remember when you got this," he said, his finger lightly tracing its outline.

"It was just a bump," she said.

"But I remember how scared I was when I saw you fall." He reluctantly lowered his hand.

Hailey looked down, a faint blush creeping up her neck.

"There's danger everywhere," Hailey said, lowering her voice, creating a cocoon of intimacy in the aisle of the store. "Statistically, driving Natasha around in your truck is more dangerous than taking her on the ski hill."

She sounded so rational and it became harder to argue with her.

"We'll be on the learner's hill. What could happen there?"

Dan realized he was being overdramatic. And Hailey's reasonable arguments made him look as though he was being stubborn for the sake of proving his point.

"Okay," he said, turning away from her. "We'll start with one day. And if Dad is feeling okay, I'm coming out to see how things go."

Hailey almost bounced, she was so pleased. "You got 'er. One day."

"So when does this start?"

Hailey bit her lip. "Tomorrow."

"Already?"

"I was hoping to ask you sooner, but then we went to the ranch and I thought I'd see how that went." She stopped and her blush grew.

They both knew how that had gone.

"Dan, I've got a customer who wants your help," Mrs. Morrow's voice called out, one aisle over.

Hailey took a quick step back, then flashed him another smile, spun around and almost skipped back to Natasha.

Her mission was obviously accomplished, Dan thought with a wry grin as he set the box down and went to help his mother.

"Make sure you dig in with one ski more than the other," Hailey said to Natasha. "Remember, like I told you, you have to make a wedge with your skis, right? Like a piece of pizza."

Natasha bit her lip, concentrating on her skis.

While she got ready, Hailey glanced up the hill. The top ridge was a white jagged edge against a hard, blue sky.

Overnight, ten inches of fresh powder had fallen up on the high runs. Hailey could see tiny, antlike figures zipping back and forth across the runs, or hurtling down others. She yearned to be there for a moment.

Hailey pulled her attention back to Natasha and the other children she was working with, Adam and Deanna. The rest of the grade one class was divided among the other four instructors. Though they'd been on the hill for almost two hours, the first half of their time had been taken up with showing the kids how to handle the equipment, taking skis on and off and the importance of safety. It was only in the past half hour that Hailey had been able to do hands-on instruction.

"Remember to keep your hands on your knees, like I showed you in the scooter drills," Hailey reminded the group. "Make your pizza with your skis as you're going down the hill. If you push harder with one ski than the other, you'll make a turn."

"Is this how I'm 'posed to do it, Miss Deacon?" Deanna called out as she slid down the hill and came to a stop in front of Hailey.

"Yes, exactly like that. Good job." Hailey clapped her gloved hands together.

Adam followed suit, also earning Hailey's praise. Finally, as if afraid of being outdone, Natasha took the plunge.

She wobbled a bit but regained control and then also came to a stop beside Adam. She shot Hailey a triumphant look and Hailey praised her loudly and effusively.

Then Natasha looked past Hailey. "Hey, Daddy. I'm skiing."

"I see that, munchkin."

Dan's voice calling out across the hill sent a light shiver dancing down Hailey's spine. She turned in time to see Dan, wearing his old snowboarding jacket, blue jeans and winter boots, trudging across the snow-covered hill to join them. His head was bare and his cheeks ruddy.

Time wheeled back and Hailey experienced the familiar surge of expectation she felt whenever they'd gone boarding together.

Where were they going today? What new jumps would they try? Would they dare to duck out of bounds?

"Miss Deacon, can we do that again?" Deanna called.

Hailey spun her head around, pulling herself back to the present. "Of course we can, Deanna. I'll go a bit farther down and you, Adam and Natasha can come ski down to me."

She ignored Dan as she demonstrated a snowplow turn to the children.

Dan stood to one side, watching as Natasha made the first attempt. She seemed far more confident. And when she came to a stop by Hailey she turned and waved to Dan. "I'm skiing lots, Daddy," she said again.

"Yes, you are," Dan said.

"Can we try the hill with the T-bar?" Adam asked.

Hailey glanced at her watch. "Sorry, Adam, I have to get you guys back to the bus in a few minutes."

"Can I stay and practice some more?" Natasha asked. "My dad can help me."

"Don't you have to go back with the other kids?" Dan asked.

"Me and Hailey came in her car," Natasha replied. "I don't have to take the bus."

"Okay, then. I'll help you."

Hailey shot Dan a thankful look, happy to see the interaction between daughter and father. Especially on the ski hill.

She took Adam and Deanna back to the rental chalet to turn in their equipment, then stayed with Megan to get the class onto the bus. When the bus had left, Hailey returned to the learner slope, pleased to see Dan and Natasha still working together.

"This is so much fun," Natasha called out to Hailey as she negotiated another turn. But in her enthusiasm, she overestimated, caught her edge too deep and fell over in a cloud of snow.

Dan immediately ran to her side, and Natasha managed to get her skis under her, only to end up sliding farther down the hill. "Stop, Natasha," Dan called, going after her. But as soon as Natasha regained control, she made another turn and scooted off in the opposite direction.

"I'm skiing, I'm skiing," she called out, her voice full of pride.

"Your dad told you to stop now," Hailey called out. The hill had such a gentle slope that if Natasha didn't stop on her own, the terrain would slow her down soon enough.

"I don't want to stop," Natasha said, keeping her hands on her knees as Hailey had showed her.

But topography worked against Natasha's wishes and a few seconds later she glided to a halt right in front of

Hailey. Dan caught up to them and the scowl on his face spoke volumes.

"You skied really good, Natasha," Hailey said before Dan could speak. "But when your dad or I tell you to stop, you have to listen."

Natasha grinned, glancing from Dan to Hailey. But when she didn't see an answering smile on either Hailey or Dan's face, her own joy seemed to fade away.

"But I wanted to ski." Natasha lowered her head.

"I know that. But in order to learn to ski properly and safely you have to learn to listen," Hailey continued, crouching down to maintain eye contact. "If you don't, we can't ski anymore."

Natasha's gaze flew from Hailey to Dan. "I don't want to stop skiing. I want to go again. Can I?"

To her surprise, a smile crept across his lips. "You can go again," he said. "But you have to listen to Miss Deacon."

"I will. I will." Natasha clapped her mittened hands together, then skied over to the Magic Carpet, the moving sidewalk that relayed her up the beginner run. As she stepped onto the plastic matting that moved up the hill, Dan walked alongside her, then watched as she got off at the top by herself.

Hailey's heart swelled at the sight. Dan, on the ski hill. Sure, it wasn't even the bunny run, but his presence showed a small acceptance of the slope.

From time to time, their eyes would meet and each time his gaze lingered a little longer. Hailey wasn't sure what was happening and right now she didn't care. They were having fun.

Just like a little family.

An hour later, Natasha's cheeks were flaming-red from exertion, Dan was slowing down and the sunlight was waning. The lifts at the top of the hill weren't running, the vacant seats swung gently up in the ever-present breeze.

The day was winding down. The liftee at the top of the hill waved to Hailey. "I'm shutting the Magic Carpet down," she announced. Hailey waved back to show her she had heard.

When Natasha made her final turn at the bottom of the hill, Hailey delivered the bad news. "It's time to go, sweetie."

To her surprise Natasha only nodded. "We had fun, didn't we?" she said, tugging her helmet off.

"We sure did." Dan brushed some snow off his knees from when he had fallen down after Natasha had run into him.

"I'm so, so hungry," Natasha said, looking from Dan to Hailey, as if expecting that they would immediately produce hamburgers or fries.

"Then we better do something about that," Dan replied. "But first we have to get you back to the rentals so you can return your skis."

"Can you please pull me, Miss Deacon?" Natasha held out a mittened hand. Hailey caught it and towed her along, snow squeaking under the hard soles of her ski boots. Natasha squealed with pleasure, Dan trailing along behind.

Fifteen minutes later the skis and boots had been returned and Dan, Hailey and Natasha walked out into the cooling air.

"So can I take Natasha here tomorrow again?" Hailey asked.

Dan looked her way and, again, a faint frisson of attraction hummed between them. Just like old times.

Even as that thought entered her head, she knew things between them had changed. Newer emotions had become part of the mix, shifting her perceptions.

"I think so," Dan said.

Hailey shoved her hands in the pockets of her jacket, releasing a smile. "Then I'll see you tomorrow," she said, taking a step back, removing herself from the two of them.

"Can we go there and get something to eat?" Natasha asked, pointing to the flashing neon sign of the restaurant beside the main chalet. "I'm so, so hungry."

"I guess we could," Dan said. "I think I have my wallet with me."

"Can Miss Deacon come with us?" Natasha said, looking from Hailey to her father. "Can she, Daddy? Can she have supper with us?"

Hailey shook her head, giving Dan an out. "I should go. You just enjoy your time together."

"No, you come with us," Natasha insisted. "You have to eat too."

"Why don't you join us?" Dan asked.

She knew she shouldn't, but the thought of returning to an empty apartment after spending such a wonderful afternoon with Natasha and Dan didn't appeal to her.

And the tender smile Dan gave her was all the encouragement she needed.

"Okay. I'll come. But I'm paying for myself," she insisted.

Dan's smile grew. "What else is new?"

She knew he referred to the fact that she had always paid her share of the bill when they were dating. "It's how I roll," she said with a casual shrug.

"I'm really hungry," Natasha repeated, in case anyone might have missed it the first time. She grabbed Hailey's hand and, leaning forward, pulled the two adults across the brick square toward the restaurant. To their left loomed the log chalet, lights streaming from inside, music pouring out the large door whenever it opened. Then a voice with a drawling New Zealand accent called Hailey's name.

"Hailey, you're finally back," a tall, lanky man exclaimed. His bright purple jacket and black snow pants made a swishing sound as he loped toward them. He stopped and swept his hair out of eyes. "Where you been? I haven't seen you in yonks."

"Erik. Wow. You're still coming here," Hailey replied, grinning at her old snowboarding friend. "I thought you would have quit years ago."

"Wouldn't miss it. It's beaut. Oh Hailey, I missed your goofy grin!" He grabbed Hailey in a tight hug and lifted her off the ground.

Erik dropped Hailey, then slapped Dan on the back. "And Dan, so good to see you too. Wow, this is brilliant. The gang is back."

"Good to see you, Erik." Dan's greeting sounded more restrained than Erik's.

Erik had shown up for the first time at Misty Ridge when Hailey was in grade ten. He had just graduated college in New Zealand and was traveling the world on his parents' dime. He came to Hartley Creek in November and stayed the entire winter, working just enough to pay for his snowboarding.

The population of Hartley Creek swelled in the winter with people like Erik. People who came to Hartley Creek from all over the world to snowboard the epic runs at Misty Ridge and work at any available job to support their passion.

Erik had connected with Dan and Hailey and had snowboarded with them whenever he could. And flirted with Hailey whenever he could. It had been a small source of tension between Dan and Hailey. She had tried to tell Dan that it meant nothing, but Dan wasn't always so sure.

Erik dropped his hands on his hips, grinning. "So, Dan and Hailey. Still together. Some things never change."

"What is he saying?" Natasha asked, before Hailey could correct Erik. "Why does he call you Den and Highly?"

Erik grinned at Natasha, then crouched down to her level. "It's me Kiwi accent, darlin'. And what's your name?"

"Nime?" Natasha asked, looking puzzled.

Hailey laughed. "Your name, honey. He's asking you what your name is."

"It's Natasha," she said, pulling a bit closer to Dan. Obviously Erik's charm was as ineffective on the daughter as it was on the father.

Erik shot his dark gaze from Dan to Hailey, then straightened, his grin growing. "So you two finally tied the knot and got a little nipper out of the deal." Before anyone could correct him, Erik clapped Dan on the shoulder. "I guess the best man did win, mate."

"We're not...not together," Dan said, slipping his arm around Natasha's shoulder.

"And what are you doing now?" Hailey asked, before Erik could make the awkward situation even more awkward. "You had an accounting degree, didn't you?"

Erik turned back to Hailey and she could see his smile shifting. "I work for myself. Just enough to pay for coming here every year. It's flash." Then he put his hand on Hailey's shoulder. "We have to go boarding again. Duck under the ropes. Take a ride on the wild side." He angled his head toward her as he gave her a slow-release smile and added a wink. Erik could turn the charm on like a tap.

"I think I'll give that a pass," Hailey returned.

"You gonna pike out on me? Too bad."

"What bed?" Natasha chimed in.

Hailey couldn't help a laugh. "You have a good evening," she said to Erik. "And enjoy the fresh powder."

"Yeah. It's gnarly." He sighed, then patted Hailey on the shoulder. "You change your mind, darlin', you know where to find me. And if you ever need company for supper, I'd be chuffed."

After sending another wink Hailey's way, Erik joined a group of people leaving the chalet, heading down the hill toward town.

"Why does that man talk so funny?" Natasha asked as they turned and walked toward the restaurant directly ahead of them.

"He's from New Zealand," Hailey explained. "They talk with a different accent. Maybe they think we talk funny too."

"I think he likes Miss Deacon. Don't you think so, Daddy?"

Dan pulled on the ski pole welded to the restaurant door as a handle. "I'm sure he does."

The edge of anger in Dan's voice puzzled Hailey. Where had that come from?

"Do you like him, Miss Deacon?" Natasha asked as the door fell shut behind them, the warmth from the stone fireplace by the door washing over them.

"He's an old friend," was all Hailey would say.

Dan shot her a frown. "So will you be going out boarding with him?"

Why was he asking?

As their eyes met, a tingle of awareness flickered down her spine.

Why did Dan care?

And this was followed by a more tentative question.

Was Dan jealous?

Chapter Nine

"Try it again," Dan called out as he double-checked the connection of the booster cables and then stood back as Hailey tried to start her car.

Dan's truck and Hailey's car were the only vehicles left on the parking lot of the ski hill. Everyone else had long gone.

Exhaust from his truck and light snow swirled around him, lit up from the beams of his truck's lights. Darkness surrounded them, broken only by a few overhead lights on the parking lot.

If he looked over his shoulder, Dan could see the lights of Hartley Creek, nestled in the valley. Home was down there. A nice warm home.

He shivered and pushed his hands deeper in his pockets. He glanced back at his truck, where Natasha still sat, making sure she was okay. For the past twenty minutes they had been trying to start Hailey's car. But now all he heard from Hailey's engine was a faint clicking sound each time she turned the key in the ignition.

She finally stuck her head out the door of her car. "I'm not getting anything."

Dan stared at the engine, as if it would give up some secret.

"Do you know what's wrong?" Hailey asked, getting out of her car.

"My guess is you need a new battery," Dan said, giving a shrug. "It should have fired up right away, hooked up to my truck."

Hailey hunched her shoulders against the gathering cold, her eyes reflecting the light from his truck. "So what do I do now?"

"I can give you a ride into town," Dan said. "We can deal with this tomorrow." If he were completely honest, the idea of spending a little more time with Hailey didn't bother him either.

They'd had a lovely dinner. Casual. Relaxed.

And thankfully Erik had stayed away.

Dan had surprised himself with the flash of jealousy he'd experienced when he'd seen Erik grab Hailey. And when he winked at her. And when he invited her to come boarding with him.

"I guess we'll have to," Hailey said. She squinted up at the falling snow. "Though it will probably have a foot of snow on it by then."

"We'll take a shovel along," Dan said. He shivered again. "But we should get going."

"Sure. You must be freezing," Hailey said, giving him a grateful smile. "Thanks for your help."

"No problem."

As Dan coiled up the cables, he glanced Hailey's way, surprised to see her still watching him. It had been that way all evening, sitting across the table from each other. A casual glance that they both allowed to linger.

The occasional brush of their hands.

It was a like a slow movement toward the emotions

they'd shared that moment in the cabin. An easy shift into different territory.

He didn't want to think too hard about what was happening. He was tired of analyzing and watching. Right now loneliness was too familiar to him and he missed having Hailey in his life.

"We should get going, then," she said, finally looking away.

She got into the truck. He tossed the cables into his toolbox, then got in himself.

"Miss Deacon's car won't start?" Natasha asked, her face lit up by the lights from the dashboard.

"No. That's why I'm taking her home," Dan said.

"You should come to our place." Natasha bounced on her seat. "We can play a game together."

"I should probably go home," Hailey said. Did she sound reluctant?

Dan dismissed his dumb thoughts with a quick shake of his head. Now he was just projecting. However, the thought of going home and spending the evening alone with Natasha held less appeal than it once had.

"Do you have games at your place?" Natasha asked.

"I don't."

"Do you watch television?"

"No. I don't have a television. Mostly I read."

That much hadn't changed. Hailey was seldom without a book of one genre or another.

"And when I know how to read, I can read books too," Natasha said. She yawned, rubbed her eyes and heaved out a sigh. "I'm glad you came skiing with me, Daddy," she said quietly, taking his hand in hers.

"I'm glad too, punkin," he replied.

And he truly was. Watching Natasha's pleasure had relaxed an ache in his heart that had been there since Austin's death. Seeing her smile as she skied and turned on the very hill that had claimed his little brother had created a small shift in his view of Misty Ridge.

As he drove no one spoke, the fresh air and exercise having taken its toll on the skiers.

Quiet strains of music came from the radio and he was content not to say anything. He saw Natasha's head bob and then she shifted, laying her head on Hailey's lap.

Dan's thoughts switched to the times he and Hailey would drive back from the hill, both of them too tired to talk. They would go up to his place, share a cup of hot chocolate and some cookies his mother had made, share stories of amazing jumps, awesome runs and excellent snow with Austin and his parents. Just before dinner, Dan would bring Hailey home.

She always said how much she hated going home. Her mother was often gone and because Naomi and Shannon had moved away, it meant she sat in her apartment by herself.

She never invited him up and he never came. It was an unspoken rule between them. A setting of boundaries.

Boundaries he'd jumped across as soon as he'd left town.

The memory of Lydia was like a stain. And a reminder?

As he came to a stop at the first set of traffic lights in town he glanced over at Hailey again, his thoughts a jumble. He knew he was treading on dangerous ground and had been from the moment he'd confessed how his relationship with Lydia had come about.

But it was as if that confession had eased a strain between them. Had that confession been a mistake? Or had he simply created a space for a change in their friendship? How would that change look?

Hailey, gently stroking Natasha's hair, shot him a sidelong glance, then slowly turned her head as their gazes connected and held.

He didn't want to look away. When a smile spread across her features and lit up her face, he couldn't.

A horn honked behind him, startling him into action. He sped through the green light, made the turn at the alley and then into the parking lot behind the store. He turned off the truck before he realized he had planned on taking Hailey home.

He was about to start the truck again when Natasha's head bobbed up. "Are we home?" she asked, stretching out her arms.

"Yes, but I have to bring Miss Deacon back to her place."

"No. Please no. I want her to come and play a game with me." Natasha turned to Dan and clung to his arm. "Please, Daddy? I won't complain about bedtime."

That was almost incentive enough. Natasha was at her most creative when trying to avoid going to bed.

"I'm sure Miss Deacon wants to go home." To an empty apartment and a book.

"Please. Just come for a little while." Natasha turned her attention to Hailey. "Daddy doesn't like to play Snakes and Ladders with me."

Hailey hesitated. "Just come up for a bit," Dan said. Reality was, he wasn't ready for her to go either. "You can help me convince Natasha that bedtime isn't the worst thing that can happen to her."

Hailey laughed. "Okay. I'll come and play a couple of games with you," she said to Natasha.

But as she spoke, her eyes were on Dan.

A few minutes later Natasha and Hailey sat in the dining room while, in the kitchen, Dan stirred hot chocolate into three mugs. He brought the steaming mugs to the table and set them down beside the girls, then sat down with Natasha.

Hailey looked at the mug beside her then shot Dan a coy look. "Did you put seven marshmallows in?"

"Exactly seven and no more," he said in a mock stern voice.

Hailey smiled, and he knew she remembered how his mother would carefully parcel out seven marshmallows per cup. She never explained why seven, only that seven was exactly enough. No more and no less.

"Four, five, six. Goody. I get a ladder," his daughter crowed, swooping her game piece up the board.

"I think I'm going to lose this game," Hailey grumbled good-naturedly.

"That's okay," Natasha consoled her. "Maybe you'll do better the next game."

Dan laughed at her parroting of the same encouragement he gave her when she was losing. Hailey's laughter wove through his and once again their gazes connected.

And once again awareness arced between them. Was it simply old feelings coming back to haunt them? Or was this something new and present?

He stifled his questions, drank his hot chocolate and allowed himself to simply enjoy the pleasure of seeing his daughter happy. Of spending time with Hailey that wasn't heavy with conflict.

Hailey and Natasha played another game and, true to Natasha's promise, Hailey won this one.

"See, I told you that you would win," Natasha said, taking a final sip of her hot chocolate. She set the cup down and glanced at Dan. "I suppose it's bedtime now," she said morosely.

"I suppose you're right."

Natasha turned her attention back to Hailey. "Can you tuck me in bed?"

Hailey opened her mouth as if to protest, then, to Dan's surprise, she simply nodded. "Sure. I think I can."

Don't read anything into it, Dan thought, getting up to grab Natasha's pajamas. *She's just humoring Natasha.* But the thought that they might share a few moments together after Natasha was in bed made him hurry up.

Be careful. Don't get involved. You have Natasha to think of.

Dan pushed the concerns away as he pulled Natasha's ruffly blue nightgown out of her drawer. Hailey was simply an old friend and he looked forward to sharing some stories with her, nothing more.

There is no "simply" with someone like Hailey. You loved her once.

Dan clutched the nightgown as he leaned against the dresser. He was tired. He was lonely. He had been dealing with a lot of changes and disruption the past few months. He hadn't had a chance to catch up with any of his old friends. This was nothing more than that.

And before his thoughts could accuse him again, he strode down the hallway to the living room to get Natasha ready for bed.

Twenty minutes and three books later Natasha scrambled into her bed and pulled the blankets around her. "Miss Deacon, you have to tuck me in," she commanded.

"Pardon me?" Dan suggested.

Natasha bit her lip. "I'm sorry, Daddy. That was rude. Miss Deacon, can you please tuck me in?"

"I don't know if I can do it right," Hailey said with a grin.

"Yes, you can. You just have to push the sheet and blanket under the mattress. And then I'm all tucked in. And then you have to sit on the bed beside me and sing my song."

"What song is that?" Hailey asked as she followed Natasha's instructions.

"The bedtime song my Daddy always sings to me." Natasha lay on the bed, the muted glow of the nightlight casting her features in shadow. But from his vantage point at the end of the bed, Dan saw her bright eyes flicking from him to Hailey, as if picking up on the sense of expectation lingering on the edges of Dan's consciousness.

"I'm in the dark here," Hailey said, sounding confused.

"Of course you are, silly," Natasha said with a giggle. "It's nighttime. Daddy, you have to start the song."

Dan cleared his throat, feeling suddenly self-conscious. He didn't have the best singing voice. But what made him the most self-aware was the fact that the song he always sang to Natasha was one Hailey had taught him.

She had taught him the song so they could sing it to their children after they were married. It was the song her grandmother had sung to her whenever she tucked her in at night.

Well, it didn't really mean anything. It was the only bedtime song he knew.

He kept his eyes fixed on his daughter as he started.

"Little one, safe in bed, God is watching your little head. God is holding your little heart, as the daylight now departs." He stopped and cleared his throat, but he sensed Hailey watching him.

He sang the other two verses and when he was done he brushed a kiss over Natasha's forehead.

"Are you sad, Miss Deacon?" Natasha asked as Dan straightened.

"It's a pretty song," Hailey replied, her voice wavering.

"My daddy said a very special lady taught it to him to sing to little kids."

"It's a good song." Hailey bent over and brushed her hand over Natasha's forehead. "'Night, sweetie," she whispered, then got up and hurried out the door.

Dan followed her out, but stopped in the doorway and waggled his fingers at his daughter, their last bedtime ritual. "Sleep well, sleep tight. Stay in your bed all night," he intoned.

"Until morning," she called back.

"Until morning," he repeated. Then he closed the door quietly behind him, waited a moment to gather his thoughts and then walked down the hallway to where Hailey waited in the dining room.

She stood with her back to him, cleaning up the game.

"I can take care of that," he said.

Her only reply was a careful sniff as her hands stilled their busy activity.

"You taught her the song," Hailey said, her voice subdued.

"It's the only bedtime song I know." Dan came to stand behind her and then, giving in to the impulse he'd been fighting all evening, put his hands on her shoulders and turned her to him.

A lone tear tracked down her cheek and the sight of it disarmed him. He could never handle tears, and Hailey cried so seldom that each instance pulled the ground out from under him.

She kept her eyes on the red game piece she was turning over and over in her hands.

"I'm sorry it made you sad," he said quietly.

She looked up at him then. "I can't believe you still remembered it."

"You sang it enough times to me," he said, eeking out a smile. "Made me memorize it."

The smile wavering over her lips lifted his heart. He gently brushed another tear away, his fingers lingering on her cheek.

"It's a good song," he said. "Natasha loves it."

"I'm glad your little girl got to hear it."

Your little girl. Not *their* child or children. The ones who were supposed to hear the song.

Regret clutched his heart. What could he say that he hadn't said already? But he couldn't let her stand there, her eyes rimmed with tears.

"I'm so sorry for how things happened," he said quietly, willing her to understand. "I'm sorry that you had to hear about me marrying Lydia from someone else."

"How could you tell me? We weren't in a good place then," she said, as if exonerating him.

Instead, it made him feel even guiltier over how things had happened after he left. And why he had left.

His heart stuttered as he pulled himself back from futile memories and mistakes that couldn't be changed. Leave the past in the past, he reminded himself. Doing otherwise served no purpose.

Right now Hailey stood in front of him, her sadness pushing at him.

"I can't change how things happened," he said, wishing he had the right words to say. "But I have to live in the present and deal with my responsibilities here and now."

"One of which is Natasha," Hailey said with a melancholy look.

"Yeah, Natasha is the biggest one and I'll do anything for her." He wished that hadn't come out like a threat. The fierceness of his love for Natasha always surprised him.

"You should be thankful for her. She's a sweet, precocious child. You're lucky to have her."

Guilt and sorrow pierced Dan like a knife. If things had gone according to his and Hailey's plan, maybe they would have a little girl by now. Or a boy. Or both.

He couldn't let himself go there. Life was what it was.

Hailey drew in a long, shuddering breath, her throat working as if she struggled to hold back her sorrow.

His fault, he thought, the knife taking a twist.

But he couldn't stand to watch her suffer anymore. He pulled her close to him, shielding her from the sadness and pain he had caused her. Tucking her head under his chin, he wrapped his arms around her, sheltering her.

"This is all a bit of a mess," she muttered against his shirt.

He had to agree. And yet, holding her close to him, he didn't feel that things were a mess at all.

For this moment, he felt as if everything was exactly right.

Chapter Ten

Hailey laid her head against Dan's chest, contentment flowing through her. It felt good to rest in his arms and be held up by him instead of being strong herself.

She stifled the warning voice telling her this was dangerous territory. How could it be? She belonged in Dan's arms.

She lifted her face and saw the broken longing in his gaze. A longing that mirrored hers.

They had lost and sacrificed enough, she thought. All she wanted from him was just one kiss. No more.

She lifted her hand, let it rest on his shoulder and then, finally, he lowered his head.

Their lips met in a slow, delicate kiss.

Dan softly drew away, his hand cupping her chin. When she saw the warmth in his eyes she realized how foolish she had been.

One kiss wasn't nearly enough.

She slipped her hand around his neck and drew him closer to her, clinging to him as if she was drowning and he was her only hope. They shared another kiss. And another.

Finally, she drew away, nestling in the cradle of his arms, wishing time would stop its steady turning.

"This feels so right," she murmured into the gentle silence cocooning them.

Dan's only reply was the slow rise of his chest as he took in a long breath. His arm held her anchored to him, his other hand rested on her head, his fingers tangling in her hair.

They stood this way for a long moment, neither wanting to be the first to break the embrace.

Then, a cough from Natasha's room brought reality into the moment.

Dan drew away, looking over his shoulder, but no sound followed the cough.

Then he turned back to Hailey, his fingers caressing her face, his eyes following their gentle path. "I feel like I should apologize, but I'm not sorry," he said.

Hailey closed her eyes, letting herself simply be in Dan's presence as the tangled and unraveled ends of her life slowly became whole.

"It just feels right," she said, catching his hand by the wrist, holding it in hers.

"It does," he agreed, pulling her close again. "I feel like I've come home after a long, hard journey."

His words settled into her heart, filling all the empty spaces that had hurt her so long.

But another cough from Natasha's room became a stark reminder of Dan's main obligation.

"I hope she's not coming down with anything," Hailey said, bringing Natasha into the moment, moving away from him.

"I think her throat is a bit raw from yelling so much today." Dan let Hailey go, but kept one hand resting on her waist, as if reluctant to release her. "She had a lot of fun. I want to thank you for that."

"And you? Did you enjoy yourself?"

Dan's slow, crooked smile told her all she needed to know. "Yeah. I did."

"I know Natasha is looking forward to going again tomorrow."

Dan brushed his fingers over her cheek. "Thanks for pushing me to let her go," he said. "You seem to know exactly what she needs. Every time."

His words created a flutter of happiness deep within her. "She's a sweet girl."

Dan looked over his shoulder, as if connecting with his daughter, then gave Hailey a rueful look.

"You know, I just realized I can't drive you home now that Natasha's in bed."

"I can walk. It's not far and I don't mind the cold."

"I'm so sorry. I wasn't thinking about how that would work for you."

It actually worked out fine, Hailey thought. But she reluctantly stepped away, unable, however, to look away. "I guess...I should be going."

Dan brushed his knuckles over her chin, then pressed another kiss to her forehead. "I'll get your coat."

Hailey wrapped her arms around herself as he left her side. She didn't want to leave, but at the same time she knew that they had played a dangerous game. Natasha was sleeping down the hall. What if she had seen them?

Would it matter?

Hailey pushed the unnerving questions aside. Natasha hadn't seen them. They didn't need to explain anything to her. Yet, as Dan returned with her coat, his eyes holding a hint of promise, she knew the situation between her and Dan had radically shifted.

The kisses they'd shared had changed everything. They couldn't go back to what they were before.

"Are you sure you'll be warm enough?" he asked as he eased her coat over her arms. "You could phone your sister and get her to pick you up."

Hailey could imagine what Shannon would make of this situation. After Dan had left the first time, Shannon had been furious with him for Hailey's sake. As a big sister she had consoled Hailey, dried her tears and told her Dan wasn't worth crying over. So what would Shannon say now, with the resentment of her own recent jilting by her fiancé still fresh in her mind?

Hailey didn't want her sister's bitterness to sully this moment.

"It's a beautiful winter night." Hailey pulled the front of her jacket together and zipped it up. "I don't mind walking for a bit." And thinking for a bit.

"Okay. But let the record show I feel really lousy about this," Dan said, stroking her hair off her face.

"Duly noted and forgiven," Hailey said, grinning up at him.

Then, to her surprise, he kissed her again. Hard. Then moved away from her to the door. "You better get going. You shouldn't be out on the streets when it's late."

"This is Hartley Creek. What could happen?" Hailey returned with a light laugh.

"Anything," was his succinct reply as he took her hand.

With reluctant steps she followed him and, when he opened the door, looked up at him again. She lifted her hand to his face, then drew away and closed the door behind her.

The air felt cool as she jogged down the stairs. At the bottom she shot a quick glance up at the windows, glowing yellow in the darkness. Dan's apartment. His parents' old home.

Hailey tugged her mittens out of her pockets, pulled them on, then headed around the building to the street.

Downtown was almost deserted, the lights casting cones of silver onto the street, illuminating the falling snow, which cooled her heated cheeks.

A few cars swished down the street, crunching through the gathering snow and as she passed the Royal, pulsating music pouring out as the door opened and people spilled out. Down the valley she heard the haunting sound of the train's horn bouncing off the hills as it came closer. It sounded again, louder this time, and Hailey heard the comforting rumble of the wheels on the tracks edging the town.

She smiled as she crossed the street at the corner. As a child the train's horn had become her way of measuring time. When she had to go home and when she had to go to sleep. It was a constant in her life and its melancholy sound seemed to underline her current emotions.

She followed the sidewalk, passing the chocolate shop with its tempting treats still in the display, the flower shop with its for-sale sign in the window and the bookstore, which held the promise of further adventures on its shelves.

She knew each business on the street and most of the owners. Though Hartley Creek could be classified as a resort town, it was coal and mining that had employed the majority of the residents for the last century. The town had its own industry, which created a solid community that didn't depend entirely on the ebb and flow of tourism.

And now Dan was a part of that community.

Dan, who had kissed her. Dan whom she had kissed back.

Hailey lifted her face, watching the heavy, fat flakes

drifting lazily down against the darkness of the sky above. Each flake fell on her face like a cool kiss.

Dan's kisses were warm.

"Oh, Lord, what have we done?" she whispered, lowering her face as she traversed the streets of her old hometown.

And yet she couldn't muster enough regret to truly feel they had made a mistake. It felt so right to be in Dan's arms and to be held by him.

Could they do this? Could they really connect again? Start over?

Her thoughts moved like a slow, gathering storm. They had loved each other once. Obviously the attraction still hummed between them. Yes, things had changed.

You have plans. You have a job waiting for you.

But all that could change and would change if…

If what? If Dan decides he can now love you again? Do you trust him to follow through? He didn't once, he might not again.

He was grieving. He made a mistake.

And could make another one.

Hailey wanted to stifle her storm-tossed thoughts. Put them to rest, but the memory of her father's desertion hung like a shadow over her life.

Dear Lord, she prayed. *Help me to understand what I should do. What Dan and I should do. I'm confused, but I'm also happy.*

And she was. Happier than she had been in a long time.

She ducked down the next street and saw her apartment as the train rumbled a block away, then receded. Tomorrow is another day, she reminded herself. See what happens tomorrow. Take things one day at a time.

"I did a good job of skiing today, didn't I?" Natasha bounced up and down on the wooden bench of the rental chalet as Hailey helped her pull her snow-encrusted boots off. "And I'm glad we went on the big hill. I wish I could go all the way up. On the chairlift."

The chalet buzzed with the excited chatter of twenty grade one students and a few tired parents who had come to help. Hailey had already assisted a number of the children with their skis while Natasha waited patiently.

"The chairlift isn't that hard to learn, but you need to be a good skier." Hailey banged the snow off the hard plastic ski boots, set them on the rubber flooring, then gave Natasha her winter boots. "Put these on, missy, and we'll bring your skis back."

"Deanna said that I am a good skier. And that she goes up on the chairlift."

"That's very nice for Deanna. You had fun with her today, didn't you?" Hailey asked.

The past couple of days Natasha and Deanna had been skiing together, laughing and racing each other down the hill. Much as she and Megan used to. Natasha and Deanna had become good friends, which boded well for next week when Hailey hoped to transition Natasha back into the classroom.

"Deanna said that she goes to the movies," Natasha added, pulling her boots on as she made a lightning-quick change in topic.

"Movies sound like fun," Hailey said, pushing herself to her feet.

"Deanna told me there was a fun movie tomorrow night," Natasha said. "Deanna said I could go with her if I wanted."

"And who is Deanna?"

Dan's deep voice behind her made Hailey jump. She turned and when she caught his smiling gaze, her own smile blossomed.

"She is my friend," Natasha replied. "She's right over there, at the desk where we bring our skis back." Natasha jumped off the bench and ran over to Dan. "Why did you come here, Daddy?"

"I had to deliver a lift of Sheetrock to the Misty Ridge Lodge. So I thought I would stop by. Give you and Miss Deacon a ride home. Especially now that we know Miss Deacon's car won't be working for a couple of days."

Hailey pulled a face. "Try a week or more. The mechanic said he could get a secondhand starter but it would take five days to get here."

"Yay for imports. Guess you'll be begging rides from me until then." Dan's grin showed her he didn't mind the idea.

"Or my sister," Hailey added.

"Can we go to the movie?" Natasha piped up. "Deanna said we should go. I never been to a movie before. Hailey said it would be fun."

"Is that what Miss Deacon said?" Dan corrected, as he swung Natasha's hand, his eyes still on Hailey.

The flush heating her cheeks surprised her. To hide her confusion at seeing him, she bent over and picked up Natasha's skis, sliding them so the bindings locked together.

She and Dan had seen each other only in passing this morning when she'd arrived at his apartment to tutor Natasha. He had to get downstairs right away to deal with an influx of customers. He hadn't come up for lunch before the school bus picked up Natasha and Hailey to take them to the ski hill. So they hadn't had a chance to experience this new place they had come to.

And now he was here.

"Can we go, Daddy? Can we? Please?"

"I think it could be fun. But we don't need to talk about that now." Dan reached over and without a word took Natasha's skis from Hailey. "I'll bring those back," he said. "Natasha, you take your ski boots please." Then he turned back to Hailey. "I'll be back." His voice held a hint of promise and an echo of what had happened yesterday.

And sent her heart knocking against her rib cage. She wished she could be calmer about the situation. Wished she didn't feel this breathless eagerness each time she was around Dan. It was confusing and disconcerting.

And it made her feel like a high school kid again.

"I have to help the kids get on the bus." Hailey poked her thumb over her shoulder at the group of children behind her.

"I can wait." His added smile didn't help her inconsistent heartbeat.

As she walked toward the gathered children she had to calm herself. Get focused. Try to put the change in their relationship in perspective.

One day at a time, she reminded herself as she helped one little boy lift his skis onto the desk.

Ten minutes later fifteen subdued and tired grade one students were lined up at the bottom of the stairs by the bus parking lot, cheeks flaming red, drooping with weariness as they waited for the bus. A few parent-helpers stood watch, chatting amongst themselves.

"So why did Dan come to pick up Natasha?" Megan asked, joining Hailey at the back of the line.

Hailey sent a quick glance over her shoulder. Dan sat on a wooden bench, Natasha on his lap as he chatted with Tim, one of the men who did repairs on the skis and snowboards. He was sitting outside, drinking a cup of coffee. Hailey recognized him as an old classmate from school.

"Just being his usual protective self," Hailey said, keeping her words purposely evasive.

"I don't know about that," Megan said in a knowing

tone. "Looks like he's paying more attention to you than Natasha."

Hailey stole another look and, just as Megan had said, though Dan had his arm around Natasha and was talking to Tim his eyes were on her. And he was smiling.

Megan caught her by the shoulder, her grin expanding. "Are you two a couple?"

"Not a couple," Hailey protested. Then, unable to keep everything tamped down, she said, "But we've spent some time together."

Megan squeezed Hailey's shoulder, barely able to contain her squeal of joy. "That's so cool. I was hoping—" She stopped herself there.

"Hoping what?" Hailey prompted, shooting her friend a puzzled frown.

Megan's eyes sparkled back at her. "Never mind."

And things came together. "You were playing matchmaker when you wanted me to tutor Natasha."

"Maybe. A little." Megan waggled her hand in a vague gesture. "And right now he is checking you out like he used to."

Hailey wished she could suppress her blush. Instead she turned her attention back to the children. "Cory, don't fall asleep, honey." She bent over and caught the little boy as he wavered on his feet. "Just hang on. Here's the bus."

And with a hiss of air brakes and crunch of tires on the snow, a long, yellow school bus pulled up in the parking lot.

The children came to life again and under the supervision of Megan, Hailey and the other parent-helpers, clanged up the metal stairs of the bus.

As the last child boarded, Dan joined her. "So, duties done here?" he asked.

Hailey watched as the doors swooshed shut behind the last adult, then nodded.

"Let's go then," he said.

But as the bus pulled away she caught Megan grinning out the window at them, giving her a discreet thumbs-up. Hailey hoped Dan didn't notice, but when she turned to go she caught his eyes flick from Megan to her.

And he was smiling.

"Can we go to the movie tomorrow, Daddy? Can we?" Natasha danced alongside Dan, hanging on to his gloved hand. His daughter's cheeks were pink from a combination of the cold air and excitement.

"Maybe," Dan said, playing along as he unlocked the door of the truck. "The store closes early on Saturday so we could."

"And Hailey can come," Natasha said before she got in the truck, her eyes shifting from Dan to Hailey and back.

Dan looked over at Hailey, who now stood beside him, her arm brushing his as she helped Natasha into the truck. "I think that might be a good idea," he said.

Kind of a clumsy way to ask her out, but Hailey's warm glance gave him hope.

"Yay. I'm so excited," Natasha shouted as she clambered into the truck.

Dan laid his arm on Hailey's, holding her back a moment. "That is, if you don't mind coming," he said, making the invitation more personal.

"I heard it was a really good movie," she said, her eyes flashing with humor.

"Four stars according to the paper," he replied.

"Sounds like a winner." Her smile grew and he felt a slow movement toward familiar territory. From the first day they'd acknowledged their attraction there had been an easy comfort between them. A sense of belonging that he never felt with anyone else.

"Are you going to stand there all day?" Natasha called out, clapping her hands like a queen summoning her subjects.

Hailey laughed and got in the truck, and as Dan walked around the front happiness mixed with anticipation bubbling up inside him.

He got in, put the truck in gear and as he headed out of the snow-covered parking lot his cell phone rang. Probably his father wondering where he was.

"Hey. What can I do for you?" he said as he spun the steering wheel of the truck toward the road.

"Dan. I'm so glad I finally connected with you."

A barb of dread hooked into his heart.

"Hello, Carla."

"I just thought I would call," Natasha's grandmother said, before he could say anything more. "See how Natasha is doing."

Checking up on him, he couldn't help thinking.

"Natasha is doing fine."

In his peripheral vision he caught Hailey's quick glance and Natasha's sudden interest.

"That's my gramma on the phone," Natasha informed Hailey in a whisper.

"We were wondering if we could come up for a visit?" Carla asked, in a deceptively reasonable tone.

Dan pulled off to one side of the road and parked. He would need all his attention for this phone call. He wished Natasha didn't have to overhear it.

Or Hailey.

"Can I call you back on this?" he said. "I'm kind of busy right now."

"Surely you can give me a simple answer."

Surely he couldn't because there was no simple answer. Natasha was settling into her life here. Having his in-laws over would disrupt the peace his daughter was enjoying and bring up old memories and pain for her.

Besides, he would be kidding himself if he thought this wouldn't become part of their campaign to get Natasha back.

He shot a quick glance over at Hailey, his mind shifting back to her conversation about the need to let Natasha deal with sorrow and Lydia's death.

But not yet, he thought. Not when things seemed to be moving to a better place in his life. He wasn't ready to analyze his and Hailey's relationship.

For now he knew it was right. And bringing Lydia back in the form of her parents would disrupt that too.

"I have to check my calendar. I'll call you back in a day or two."

"If we don't hear from you, then I'll call you as well," Carla said.

Dan tried not to see that as a threat. But as he hung up on her, he had to suppress a sense of foreboding.

He slammed his truck in gear and spun down the road.

"Everything okay?" Hailey asked.

Dan sucked in a deep breath, then backed off on the accelerator. No sense in getting themselves plowed into the ditch.

He eased out a tight smile. "Sure. Just fine. I'll bring you home and call you tomorrow about the movie. Maybe pick you up early and we could go for pizza?"

"That sounds like a great idea," Hailey said.

Natasha squealed with excitement. "Yay. We're going to have a pizza and movie night. That's rad."

Dan and Hailey both laughed and as they drove Hailey

home he forced himself to relax. He didn't have to think about Carla and Alfred right now.

Help me, Lord, to take one day at a time, he prayed, *and to enjoy the day I have right now.*

Because no matter what, he couldn't suppress a sense of foreboding that, once Lydia's parents came to Hartley Creek, everything would change for the worse.

Chapter Eleven

"Do you think it will be a good movie? I hope it has a princess in it." Natasha wiggled in her seat, almost spilling the tub of popcorn on her lap.

"I don't think it does," Hailey said, pulling Natasha's tangled ponytail straight. All day Natasha had been taken care of by a young girl in high school but it seemed hair care wasn't one of Colleen's strengths.

"I don't mind. I think it will be fun no matter what." Natasha's gaze was riveted on the pictures flashing on the screen—advertisements and trivia games—and Hailey glanced over her head.

Dan grinned back at her and laid his arm across the back of Natasha's seat, his fingers within centimeters of her shoulder.

A light flutter of anticipation began in her midsection. Just as it had when she and Dan had gone to the movies. Except then they sat side by side, Hailey would lean her head on his shoulder and his arm reached all the way around her.

"Oh. Oh. I think it's starting," Natasha squealed, leaning forward as the lights dimmed. Sound blasted from the speakers surrounding them and images flickered on the screen.

They watched the trailers for upcoming movies and then, finally, the main feature started.

Anticipation curled in her middle as the movie studio logo came up with its triumphant music. How often had she and her sisters and cousins come here clutching their spare cash? Their entrée into other worlds—sailing across oceans with pirates, heading off into space, flying on horses across open plains—each adventure more amazing than the last.

Then, when she was older, tucked up against Dan's side living through drama, action, adventure and romance.

Dan's fingers brushed her shoulder. His touch was so light she might have imagined it. But sitting in the dark, with only his daughter between them, she had become hyperaware of his every movement.

She caught the sparkle of his eyes looking over at her.

They were flirting with each other. No other word for it.

And where would this go? What could come of it?

She quenched the annoying questions, lifted her hand and laid it against his, anchoring it to her shoulder.

But as they sat in the dark, connected, she knew they would have to talk about this. They weren't careless teenagers anymore, testing the waters of affection and attraction.

Natasha's presence was a potent reminder of what was at stake.

In spite of her reservations, Hailey kept her hand covering Dan's rough one as images flickered on the screen in front of them, a kaleidoscope of color and sound melding past and present. From time to time his hand would shift and she would look his way and they were young kids all over again.

Stolen glances, gentle touches.

She wished she could dismiss the swirling undercurrents. Wished she could simply pull her hand away and return to being Hailey Deacon, woman with a plan to leave.

But couldn't that plan change? Could she and Dan become what they once had been? Could she stay here?

As if he'd read her thoughts, Dan's hand slid below her hair and his fingers made slow, entrancing circles on the back of her neck. Just as he used to.

One day at a time, she reminded herself as shivers slipped up and down her spine.

All too soon the closing credits flowed up the screen. The houselights came up and Dan pulled his hand away from hers. Hailey blinked in the growing light and Natasha sat back in her chair, her expression rapt.

"That was so, so fun," she said, her voice quiet with awe. "Way better than television."

Hailey shot Dan a grin as she helped Natasha with her coat. "I'm guessing this is only the beginning of a whole new adventure."

"I can see my Saturday evenings flashing before my eyes."

"In Technicolor and surround sound," Hailey joked.

"Did you like the movie?" Natasha asked Hailey as she zipped closed the coat.

"It made me laugh," was all Hailey could say, because Dan had held her attention more than the story line playing out on the screen.

"I liked the part where the mouse said, 'Oh, no you don't, you rascal,' that was so, so funny," Natasha said, suddenly overcome with another fit of the giggles. "What part did you like the best, Hailey?"

As her mind scrambled for something she caught Dan's

eye and saw his mouth quirk upward. He knew she was distracted but she wasn't letting him off easy.

"Why don't you ask your daddy what he liked the best?"

"Touché," was all he said, then he bent over to retrieve Natasha's popcorn bucket. "Do you want to keep this, munchkin?" he asked.

"I'm full," she said, placing a greasy hand on her stomach. "Can we watch the movie again tomorrow?" Natasha asked. "They said they are going to have it again tomorrow afternoon."

"We have church—"

"We have church tomorrow—"

As Hailey replied at the same time as Dan, she felt a flash of self-consciousness. She was Natasha's tutor, not her mother.

But the lines between the two were blurring. Which lent urgency to discussing their relationship. A little girl who'd had a lot to deal with was involved and they had better tread warily.

The thought was a sobering douse of cold water and Hailey turned away from Dan, moving out into the crowded aisle, joining the people leaving the theater.

"Hailey Deacon. Hold up a minute."

A familiar voice called out and Hailey turned in time to see Mia Verbeek, an old school-friend of hers, waddling up the aisle. Her short brown hair framed her face in a cute pixie cut. She looked sixteen but the four-year-old boy tugging on one hand and her mounded stomach proclaiming an advanced pregnancy told a different story.

"Hey, how are you doing?" Hailey asked, smiling at the sight of Mia.

"Same as last time I saw you. Pregnant," Mia said, pushing down on her stomach with one hand with a groan. "But we plug along."

"Where's Josh?"

"He's sick so I left him with my mom. Nico really, really wanted to come to the movie and I couldn't hit the matinee, so here we are."

"Hey, I heard rumors that you're buying the flower shop?" Hailey said, shuffling along with the crowd, leaving Dan and Natasha behind. "That's pretty ambitious." And puzzling. The last time she and Mia had coffee together, Mia was content to stay at home with her two boys, being a homemaker, a wife to Dean and getting the nursery ready for her twin girls.

"Girl's gotta do what a girl's gotta do," was Mia's ambiguous reply. Mia glanced back at the people coming up behind them. "So, I noticed you and Dan sitting together." Mia gave Hailey a broad wink. "Just like old times."

Hailey's mind shifted back to Natasha sitting between Dan and Hailey, a visible reminder of how different from old times their situation had become. "Not really. I'm just tutoring his daughter."

Mia playfully punched Hailey's shoulder with a fist. "You and Dan are like peanut butter and jam. I couldn't believe it when I found out he was back the same time you were, and now look at you two. I think you might be changing your mind about that job you were talking about," she added with a knowing grin.

Hailey felt a small lift of panic at the thought of her future changing because of what was happening between her and Dan. Did she dare change her plans? And if she didn't, what was she doing to Dan and Natasha?

Hailey pushed the future aside and gave Mia a quick grin. "I'm not making any plans one way or the other yet."

They reached the end of the crowded aisle and the crush of bodies dissipated as people moved into the foyer.

Mia's son, Nico, tugged on her arm, dancing from one

foot to the other. "I have to go to the bathroom," he announced.

"Of course you do, after all that pop you drank. Hang on a few more seconds." Mia turned back to Hailey, her expression growing serious. "Speaking of plans, I'd love to get together with you again. I need... I just would like to visit with you."

Hailey frowned at the suddenly serious tone of her friend's voice. "Yeah. Sure. Just say when."

"Mommy. Please."

"I'll call you," Mia said, waggling her fingers at Hailey as she walked across the lobby, her son pulling her along.

"Was that Mia Strombitsky?" Dan asked, as he caught up to her, Natasha clinging to his hand.

Hailey looked back, unable to stop the silly flicker of her heart when their eyes connected.

"Yeah. Except she's Verbeek now. I hung out with her in high school. She's married now. Expecting twin girls."

"And I heard she has two boys already. That's a lot of kids," Dan said with a laugh as they walked into the foyer.

And as Hailey watched Mia negotiate the bathroom door a faint twinge of envy caught her. She'd always wanted lots of kids. Mia was the same age and already had four.

Hailey was still single and had none.

"Are you coming to our house again?" Natasha asked as they walked toward the outside door. "Are you tucking me in again and singing the special sleeping song?"

Hailey smiled down at the little girl as something deep and maternal moved through her.

"I'd like it if you came," Dan's deep voice added.

That was all she needed to hear.

A blast of cold, dark air greeted them as they stepped out of the warm movie house. Snow drifted down onto the cars parked in the parking lot of the movie theater, sparkling in the light cast by the streetlamps.

The air looked magical and as Hailey walked with Dan back to the truck, anticipation buzzed through her.

On the short drive back to the apartment, Natasha filled the silence with animated chatter about the movie, her favorite characters and what she would do if she ever met a talking mouse.

An hour and two cups of hot chocolate later, Natasha was tucked in her bed, cheeks shining from her bath, eyes glowing as she looked from Dan to Hailey. "And now you have to sing the song."

"Yes, your majesty," Hailey joked, settling down on one side of the single bed, Dan on the other. She rested her hand on the opposite side of Natasha and when Dan did the same, it was as if they created a sanctuary for the little girl.

And created a connection between her and Dan.

As they sang the song, Hailey felt her heart filling with a peculiar emotion. Affection for the little girl, but something deeper. Stronger.

Love.

Her voice faltered on the words, eliciting a puzzled frown from Dan. He shifted his hand to rest on her knee, giving it a light squeeze that did little for her equilibrium.

And as his eyes met hers, a promise glowed in their depths.

They got to the last verse and Dan's cell phone rang, bursting into the intimacy of the moment.

"Sorry," he mumbled as he pulled his phone out of his pocket and beat a hasty retreat.

Hailey finished the song, tucked the blankets around Natasha just the way she liked them, then giving in to an impulse bent over and kissed Natasha on the forehead.

It was the first time she had kissed the little girl and when she drew back, Natasha's eyes glowed.

"I love you, Miss Deacon," she said, suddenly sitting up and throwing her arms around her.

Her words were at one time both heartwarming and painful. Even while her declaration created an ache of yearning in Hailey's heart, it immediately made her think of what Natasha had lost. Lydia's death was the reason Natasha had attached to her so quickly.

Be careful, a voice warned her. *Tread very carefully with this little girl.*

Because she knew whatever she decided she would do in the future would have an impact on Natasha and her well-being.

"I don't think it will take her long to fall asleep," Dan said as he walked back to the living room.

Hailey stood in the center of the room, her hands fiddling with the ends of her scarf, as if uncertain what she should be doing. "That's good."

"Sorry about that phone call," he said, tossing his phone onto an end table in the living room. "Turns out I should have let it ring," he said with a heavy sigh.

"Bad news?"

He shook his head as he dropped onto the couch. He was thankful when Hailey followed suit.

He wasn't ready for her to go home. He wanted to spend some time, just the two of them. Just like old times.

"Actually, that was Natasha's other grandparents again. Lydia's parents. When they called yesterday I said I would call back, but things got busy today and I forgot. I knew they wouldn't." He shoved his hand through his hair, then dropped his arm along the back of the couch, his hand landing inches from Hailey's shoulder.

"What did they want?"

A weary sigh slipped out. "To visit Natasha."

"You don't sound pleased with the idea," Hailey said, tucking her feet under her.

"I don't know what to do about it. Natasha is still getting settled. I'm worried that them coming here will cause more problems."

Hailey twirled a strand of hair around her finger, her lips pursed.

"You look like you don't agree," Dan said.

"Your parents really enjoy having her around."

"They're thrilled. They hardly got to see her when she was little. It was hard enough for me to get my regular visits, let along bring her back here."

Hailey nodded, smiling. "They do dote on her."

"My father would give her every toy in the store if he had his way and my mother can't stop hugging her."

Hailey laughed, then lowered her hand, letting it rest on his. Her skin felt cool, soft, as he twined his fingers in hers. He wished his weren't so rough. "I know how much my grandparents loved us kids," she said, her voice quiet. "I remember my Nana telling me she would have done anything for us."

"And you would do anything for her," Dan said, tightening his grip on her hand.

"When I heard about her heart attack I couldn't come back fast enough. I love her so much and can't imagine what my life would be like without her." Hailey gave him a trembling smile. "But at the same time, I sometimes wonder about my father's parents. Why they didn't contact my mother. I often wondered if they even cared about me and my sisters." She stopped there, biting her lip, looking away.

"You've never heard from them?"

"I've never heard from my father."

Her bitter tone surprised Dan. Hailey had never spoken of her father and Dan only knew that he had left her mother when Hailey was about eight.

"I used to wonder if they ever thought about us or wanted to see us." She pulled her hand away, lowering it to her lap.

The hitch in her voice surprised him. Hailey was always so tough. So sure of herself. But in the past few days he'd seen her cry. Twice. And now he was learning things that he'd never known before.

"I'm so sorry," he said, moving closer to her, putting his hand on her shoulder. "I never knew that."

"You don't need to feel sorry for me. I don't. It's just part of my reality." Hailey released a laugh, but kept her eyes down. "I think it's important, however, that Natasha doesn't have to deal with the same questions. The more people she has in her life that love her, the more secure she'll feel."

Dan blew out a sigh. "That makes sense, but I'm worried about the Andersons. They've been fighting for custody of Natasha ever since Lydia died. They're not scared to toss money toward a lawyer if it means getting Natasha back. Carla has never made a secret of the fact that they want Natasha."

"That's too bad," Hailey said. "It's sad when families resort to fighting instead of talking things through."

"For now, though, I think it's best if they keep their distance. They've seen enough of Natasha before, when Lydia had custody of her. I had to fight for every minute I spent with my own daughter. I'm not about to let that happen again." Dan let his hand rest on Hailey's shoulder, shifting himself a bit closer. "But I don't want to talk about the Andersons right now."

Hailey tilted her head to one side, her smile showing him her willingness to go along with the change in topic. "What do you want to talk about?"

Dan let his fingers twine in her hair as his other hand caught hers. "I think we both know something is happening between us. We've been here before."

"And yet it's different," Hailey said, finishing his thoughts like she used to.

"A lot different." He stroked her hand with his thumb, making gentle circles as he tried to find exactly the right words.

Then Hailey tossed her hair back and looked directly at him, holding his gaze. "Do you ever wonder where we would be if things had been... If things hadn't happened the way they did?"

"I tried not to. But lately it's been harder."

"Why?"

"Because I see you every day. And every day I'm reminded of what I lost."

He moved closer, sliding his hand up her arm, capturing her shoulder. "I'm so sorry for the way things turned out," he said. "But you need to know I've never forgotten about you. I thought about you all the time."

"But when I saw you that first time, you seemed so angry. So remote." The confusion on her face was mirrored in her voice.

Dan touched her cheek with his forefinger, as if she was a bird that could take flight if he made the wrong move or said the wrong thing.

"I had to be that way. I had to protect myself."

"From me?"

"From what I felt for you." He stroked her face, then shifted his hand around the back of her head. "From what I knew I lost when I left."

"I'm glad you told me about Lydia," she said, stroking his arm. "It changed a lot for me. Explained so much."

"I was scared and I missed you like crazy." He didn't want to talk anymore. Words were getting in the way. He pulled her close and kissed her gently. She returned his kiss and then rested against him, cradled against his chest, held close in his arms.

This was how it should be, Dan thought, easing out a sigh as he pressed a kiss to her temple.

"I don't know the right words to use," he finally said, "but I feel like this is right. Having you in my arms, well, it feels like home."

He could feel her smile.

"I know what you mean."

They sat quietly, enjoying the moment.

Then, she pulled away, her expression serious.

"So where do we go from here?" she asked, folding her hands over each other.

"I'd like to say we can take it one day at a time," he replied, knowing they needed to have this discussion. "But I don't know if I have that luxury."

"Your life is more complicated now because of Natasha," Hailey said, voicing the words for him again.

"I have to think about her. She's my first priority."

He didn't know what else to say. Didn't know where they were supposed to go from here. They couldn't go back to the place they were before—two kids making all kinds of plans. They had to deal with the issues between them.

"I don't want to lose you again," Hailey finally said.

"I don't want to lose you either."

"Then we have no choice *but* to take this one step at a time," Hailey said quietly. "But to always keep Natasha's well-being our first priority."

Dan nodded. What Hailey said was sensible and mature. They had a plan.

So why did he feel as if he was missing something?

Chapter Twelve

"How did things go today?" Dan bent over and picked up Natasha's backpack from the floor of the school's hallway.

"Really well, didn't they, Natasha?" Hailey asked as she zipped up Natasha's coat.

Natasha nodded. "I made a clay mountain today," she said, demonstrating with her hands.

"And you did a good job," Hailey said.

Behind them a couple of children ran down the hall toward the double doors, screaming for the bus to wait, the excitement of Friday adding a shrill note to their voices.

"Tell your daddy what else you did today," Hailey said as she handed her toque and mitts to the little girl.

"I wrote in my journal. And Miss Tolsma is going to write back to me," Natasha beamed as she tugged on her toque and shoved her mitts in her pocket.

On Monday morning when Hailey had come to the apartment to teach Natasha, she had floated the idea of Natasha coming to school for a few mornings. Thankfully, Natasha had been excited about the idea. Then on Thursday she had decided, on her own, that she wanted to start coming for the full day on Friday, today.

However, that meant it was also the first day Hailey had

seen Dan only for a few moments, this morning when he'd dropped Natasha off at school and now.

As Hailey straightened she glanced Dan's way. "Do you have a plan for her care after school?" she asked. Though they had seen each other every day, Hailey knew things would change for her and Dan once Natasha attended school every day.

"I asked Colleen, the girl that took care of Natasha last week, to come after school as well as Saturday," Dan said as he took Natasha's hand.

"That's good. I'm glad things are coming together." Though she had to admit she felt left out of the loop.

"They are, but, well, I missed you today," he said quietly, speaking thoughts aloud that she'd had of him too.

Hailey glanced at Natasha, who was looking straight ahead, seemingly lost in her own thoughts, then she looked back at Dan, her heart warming at his crooked smile and intent gaze.

"I missed you too," she said quietly.

"Do you want to come over for supper tomorrow night? Mom brought me a couple of casseroles today and I've got more than enough for the three of us."

"Tomorrow?" Hailey couldn't keep the disappointment out of her voice. "I promised my Nana and my sister I'd go out for supper with them. It's Shannon's birthday."

His expression mirrored her feelings.

"But I can come Sunday," she added.

Natasha snapped out of wherever she was. "Sunday? I want to go skiing Sunday."

"Sorry, honey," Dan said. "I am busy after church and can't take you."

"Hailey can take me." Natasha turned to Hailey with a winning smile. "Can you?"

Hailey looked down, recognizing the same breathless

enthusiasm that had sent her, whenever she could scrape together enough money for a lift ticket, to Misty Ridge.

"I'm not busy," she said, but then glanced at Dan to make sure it was okay before she offered to take Natasha. The reluctance on his expression was a bit of a puzzle to her. "But maybe your daddy wants you to spend time with your gramma."

"I see Gramma all the time. Please, Daddy, can I go?" Natasha turned to Dan, pulling on his hand. "Then Hailey can take me home and we can have supper. Please, Daddy?"

Natasha scrunched up her face in the same pleading gesture Hailey had been subjected to from time to time.

Dan bit his lip, obviously reluctant, which puzzled her.

Then Natasha turned her pleading gaze toward Hailey. "Please tell my daddy to let me go."

Hailey held up her hands, giving Dan an out. "I'm not getting involved. If your daddy doesn't want me to take you, then that's the way it is."

Dan looked as if he was about to say something when Natasha pulled on his hand again.

"I'll be really good and I'll eat all my casserole tomorrow night and I won't spit out the mushrooms."

Hailey suppressed a laugh and even Dan's expression lightened.

"Okay. You can go," he finally conceded.

"Yay, yay, yay," Natasha called out, pumping the air with a fist, then released Dan's hand and danced around Hailey. "We can go skiing again. We can go skiing again." The little girl leaned against Hailey, looking up at her. "And then Sunday night you can come for supper because you can't come Saturday. And you can stay and sing me a song. And then you can kiss my daddy again."

Hailey went cold and taut at Natasha's words, her gaze flying to Dan's.

He looked equally shocked. She saw him swallow, as lost for words as she was.

"I saw you," Natasha said, frowning as if she didn't understand the moment of surprise holding Dan and Hailey in its thrall. "And it made me happy."

Well, that was a small blessing, Hailey thought. But still.

Dan pulled his hand over his face, then blew out his breath. He looked as surprised and agitated as Hailey felt.

"So are you coming Sunday?" Natasha asked, taking charge of the awkward moment. "You can come and pick me up after church."

"I guess so, now that it's okay with your daddy." Though she still sensed his reluctance.

Dan took Natasha's hand, then shot Hailey a quick glance. "So we'll see you Sunday after church?"

"I'll be by at about one," Hailey said.

He hesitated a moment, then said, "We need to talk."

She guessed he alluded to Natasha's little revelation and nodded. "Sunday evening."

"It'll be okay." Dan brushed his finger over her cheek, his light touch even more reassuring than his smile. "See you then."

As they walked away from her, and the door closed behind them, Hailey was surprised at the sudden jittery feelings gripping her.

She dismissed her concerns with a shake of her head. Sunday she would be spending time with Natasha. And then she would be having dinner with Dan and Natasha.

Just like a little family.

The thought erased the misgivings in her soul. Things were moving along step by step and they were moving to a good place.

* * *

"Are you sure you don't want dessert?" Hailey asked her grandmother from across the table in the noisy restaurant. Carter, Hailey's cousin, sat beside Nana and Emma sat beside him.

They looked happy, Hailey thought, watching as Carter bent his head toward Emma's darker one to catch what she said. Hailey's own happiness made it easier to watch the two lovebirds.

"I'm quite full," Nana said, "And until I can start walking more frequently, I had better watch my caloric intake."

"That might be a while before you can go walking regularly," Carter said, raising his head. "I heard the snow will be around until end of March."

Shannon shivered. "That sounds depressing. When I move, I'm going somewhere warmer."

"Move?" Nana perked up at that.

"In spite of not being able to walk, you've been feeling pretty good, haven't you?" Hailey asked her grandmother, making a quick switch in topic. Neither Shannon nor Hailey had told their Nana about their potential moves, knowing how much their plans would upset her.

Though Hailey was sure she wouldn't be moving anywhere.

We need to talk. Dan's words echoed in her mind, reassuring and mysterious at the same time.

"I'm feeling a bit tired yet, which disappoints me," Nana said, glancing around the table. "But sitting here in the restaurant with my grandchildren and grandchild-to-be makes my heart very happy." Nana turned her attention to her oldest granddaughter. "I'm so glad we could do this for your birthday, Shannon, and I hope we can do this many, many more years."

"I'm glad we could do this too," was all Shannon would say.

Hailey knew the reason for her evasive reply. If things went the way Shannon wanted, she would be gone once all the cousins made their way back to Hartley Creek. She had gotten a job as a travel nurse and was moving to Chicago. Hailey had been surprised her sister had taken the job. Up until a year ago Shannon had loved her job working as an emergency room nurse. Of course, she had also loved her fiancé, Arthur, until he'd called off the wedding two weeks before the date. The shame of that public humiliation had Shannon packing up to leave town. If it hadn't been for Nana's heart attack, Shannon would have been long gone.

And what about the job waiting for you? Hailey brushed the question aside. She wasn't doing anything about future plans until after Sunday. When she and Dan would have their "talk."

The buzz of conversation around them created lulling background noise. Beside their table sat a couple still wearing their ski jackets and pants, conversing in German. Across from them, a group of young people wearing the funkier clothing of snowboarders chattered about their exploits on the hill that day, various accents sparkling in their earnest conversation.

"I missed this," Hailey mused aloud, her hands wrapped around the oversize mug of tea.

"Missed what?" Carter asked, pulling a toothpick out of its plastic wrapper.

"The ambience of this town in the winter. All the different types and nationalities of people that come here to ski and board."

Shannon glanced around the restaurant and Hailey saw a melancholy smile drift across her sister's mouth. "Yeah. I know what you mean."

"Things certainly have changed in this town since I was young," Nana said with a slow shake of her well-coiffed head as she looked around the busy restaurant. "I remember when there weren't nearly as many places to eat or hotels and most of the people that lived in this town were connected to the coal industry or the railroad."

"Lots of people still are," Hailey assured her. "It's a strong community. A good place to live."

This netted her a wry look from Shannon and Hailey guessed her sister would be asking her about her comment when she brought Hailey home.

"Speaking of places to live, have you started looking yet?" Shannon asked her Nana.

Since her heart attack, Nana had been looking at leaving the ranch she had moved onto as a young bride and purchasing a house in town. But to date, she hadn't found anything.

"I'm in no rush," Nana said. "But I don't want to talk about a house just yet. For now, I'm glad we could spend this time together," Nana said with a gentle look for each of her grandchildren. "Though I think it's time for this old lady to get home."

She lifted a finger to indicate that she wanted the bill.

Their waiter sauntered over, a study in indifference. "So ladies, is there anything else I can get you?" he asked, his tattooed hand resting on his hip, both eyes resting on Shannon.

"I'd like the bill," Nana said briskly, obviously unimpressed with his easygoing attitude.

"Of course," he said with one more lingering look at Shannon, then left.

"The service is getting entirely too casual here," Nana sniffed. "And I don't like the way he flirted with you, Shannon."

Hailey nudged her sister with her elbow. "I don't think Shannon minded that much."

Shannon shot her sister an oblique look. "Not interested."

When their waiter returned, Nana and Carter had a mini tussle over the bill but Nana won out, as she always did.

Ten minutes later Hailey and Shannon were waving Carter's truck off, its taillights blinking at the intersection. Then watched it turn onto the road leading to the highway that would take them home.

"That was nice," Hailey said as she pulled her coat around her. A sudden wind had picked up, sending chilly fingers snaking down her back.

"I'm so glad to see Nana looking so much better," Shannon said, pressing the button on her keychain to unlock her car, which was parked down the street from the restaurant.

"She seems a lot happier, though I think a lot of that is just because she's got most of us around for now." Hailey ducked into Shannon's compact car and shivered as Shannon started it up. "I'll be so glad when my own car is fixed," she announced, her breath a white fog in the cold interior of the car.

"When is it ready?" Shannon asked as she put her car into gear. Her wheels spun, then gained traction as she turned onto the street.

"Monday. So I was wondering if I could borrow your car tomorrow. I'm taking Natasha to the ski hill."

Shannon shot her an oblique look. "You seem to be spending a lot of extracurricular time with Dan," Shannon returned.

Hailey hunched her shoulders, her hands buried in her pockets, wishing she didn't feel she had to defend herself. "I am still Natasha's tutor."

"Yeah, but you're not Dan's girlfriend anymore. And

you used to talk as badly about Dan as I talk about Arthur the snake."

The only sound following her sister's comment was the squeaking of tires on the snow and the hum of the car's heater fan. Hailey knew Shannon was simply watching out for her, but she didn't want to hear her own misgivings spoken aloud.

"I'm just telling you to be careful," Shannon said, turning the fan down. "He's a guy and we both should know by now guys can't be trusted."

"I was the one that broke up with Dan before he left, remember?"

"Only because you wanted to beat him to it. Remember?"

Hailey did. After Austin's funeral Dan had retreated so far from her she'd known in only a matter of time he would finally sever their fragile connection before he moved away.

"It's different now." She spoke the words quietly, as if unsure of the strength of her emotions. "I feel such a strong connection to him. It just feels...it feels right."

"Feelings are all well and good, but you need to be smart about this," Shannon said as she turned onto the street leading to Hailey's apartment. "He broke your heart once before and you didn't even know why."

"It was because of Austin."

Shannon slowed and parked in front of Hailey's apartment. She looked ahead, her lips puckered in an expression of concern. Then she turned to Hailey, her long hair framing her face, the light from the dashboard casting her wide eyes and narrow nose into shadow.

"You know, I always thought that was a lame excuse on his part. He lost a brother, but you lost a good friend too. You were grieving too." Shannon was quiet, as if expecting Hailey to respond to that. "Has he said anything about why he left? What his real reasons were?"

Hailey pressed her fingers to her forehead. She didn't want to be confused or to go back to that horrible time when it had seemed as if her heart had been cut out of her chest.

"That's in the past. Why go there?"

"Because sometimes you need to go back before you can go ahead," Shannon said.

Her words struck a chord deep within Hailey's heart. She knew her sister was right. "But things are going so well." Hailey turned to her sister, feeling as if she had to explain. "I never cared for someone the way I care for Dan," she said. "You know that. I tried dating other guys, but it was never the same. Now, being with him, I feel like I'm whole again."

"And what about his daughter?"

"I think she really cares for me too."

Shannon's doubtful expression didn't shift one centimeter.

"I'm happy now," Hailey said, willing her sister to understand. It was as if she needed Shannon's blessing to eradicate the concerns roaming the deepest recesses of her mind. "Happier than I've been in a long time. Surely that has to mean something?"

"I think it does," Shannon finally said, reaching over and covering Hailey's hand, granting her a bit of reassurance. "But I'm just telling you to be careful. You really don't know why he left, or why he felt he had to leave. I think you need to find out more about what happened before you move on. Besides, you have Natasha to think about. If this doesn't work out, it could be devastating for her."

Hailey nodded, knowing her sister was right.

Then Shannon squeezed her hand. "I'll be praying for you."

Hailey eked out a smile. "Thanks for that."

"I'll stop by tomorrow morning. You can bring me to work and then the car is yours the rest of the day."

"Thanks, sis." Then Hailey stepped out of the car, the chilly air cooling the heat of her cheeks. She fumbled in her purse for her keys, and when she had them in her grasp she turned and waved at her sister.

Shannon waved back, tooted the horn and drove away.

But as Hailey walked up the flight of stairs to her apartment, Shannon's words resounded in time to each footfall echoing in the stairwell.

Be careful. Be careful.

Chapter Thirteen

"You got everything you'll need?" Dan asked, handing Hailey an extra pair of bright red mittens with white maple leaves on them. "Snacks? Extra socks?"

Hailey nodded as she stuffed the mittens into the backpack sitting on the floor of the apartment's front entrance. "I think we're well provided." As their eyes met he caught an excited sparkle in her gaze.

He and Natasha had slept in this morning and missed church. As a result he'd been dogged with guilt all morning. But underneath his guilt crept an uneasiness that had nothing to do with missing church and everything to do with Natasha going on the ski hill with Hailey. But he had to let her go. He didn't want Hailey to think he didn't trust her with his daughter. Especially not after allowing her to go with the class.

That was different. That was an organized trip.

Dan shoved his hand through his hair, then grabbed the back of his neck. "Okay, then. I guess you should get going."

"Not yet," Natasha called out, lurching to her feet, her movements hampered by her snow pants and coat. "I have to get my wings."

"You won't need them, honey," Dan said, shooting Hailey a pleading look to help him out.

"But they'll help me ski better," Natasha complained, already heading off to her bedroom.

"One of these days she's got to stop wearing those silly things," Dan muttered as she left.

"I'll let her wear them for a couple of runs, then convince her she can ski without them," Hailey assured him. "She doesn't wear them to school, so that's a good thing."

"I suppose I should be thankful for small blessings," Dan said.

Hailey zipped up the backpack and stood. "So, I'm ready to go."

Dan nodded, his previous misgivings returning. "So you'll be careful, right?" The question burst out before he could think about it.

Hailey's light frown bothered him, but he couldn't help himself.

"Of course I will."

Still he hesitated.

"She'll be okay," Hailey said. "Please don't worry about her. I'll take care of her like she was my own."

Dan experienced a precarious happiness and, at the same time, a thrum of concern. He and Hailey. Was he making a mistake?

But as his eyes held hers, he felt that what was happening between him and Hailey was right and true.

He also knew that since he'd kissed Hailey, the restlessness that had been his constant companion since he'd left Hartley Creek had settled.

Hailey glanced past him, then her expression grew even more serious. "Has she said anything more about...about what she saw?"

"You mean us kissing?"

"Yeah. That."

"No. And I haven't had a chance to talk to her about it." He heard Natasha rattling around in her drawers and decided to let her root around on her own for a few more moments. He turned back to Hailey, trying to figure out the best way to express what he wanted to say.

And at that moment her cell phone rang.

Hailey drew it out of her pocket, glanced at it, then turned away from Dan to answer it.

"Yes. This is Hailey Deacon.... Oh, hello. No, it's fine to call me now. I realize you're probably busy during the week." She shot Dan a look of concern, then took a few steps farther into the house, going around a corner.

To give her some privacy he went back to Natasha's room to help her out. The room was an explosion of clothing and toys. "What happened here?" he asked Natasha, who was on her knees, head in her closet, as she tossed clothes and shoes over her shoulder.

"I can't find them," her muffled voice called out, close to panic. "They were from my mommy and I can't find them."

Dan walked over to the closet and pulled Natasha to her feet with a swish of her snow pants. Her face was beet-red and her hair a damp tangle. Poor kid was cooking-hot, wearing her ski clothes in the house.

"I think you left them in the bathroom the last time you wore them," he said. "In the cupboard where the towels are."

Natasha sniffed and when she grinned Dan knew she remembered too. "Thanks, Daddy. I don't want to lose them. They came from my mommy and they are special."

Her comment about Lydia brought up his misgivings. He felt as if he and Hailey hovered on the cusp of something that would change everything for his daughter. He needed to know where Natasha was emotionally before he and Hailey made any kind of commitment.

The word resounded in his mind as he knelt down, looking directly into his daughter's eyes.

Commitment. Was he ready? Were he and Hailey really heading in that direction? He tested the thought as he brushed a few strands of hair back from his daughter's red face.

"Honey, remember you said that you saw me and Miss Deacon kissing?"

Her expression shifted and she gave him what could only be described as a flirty grin. "Yes. I did," she said, clasping her hands in front of her and twisting back and forth.

"How did you feel about that?"

Natasha lifted her shoulders and giggled. "I felt happy." Then she leaned closer, whispering. "Are you and Miss Deacon in love?"

How did she know this stuff?

"We like each other" was all he could say for now. He didn't know if he dared mention love yet. Not in front of his daughter and not even to himself.

As for Hailey, there were moments he was sure she sensed his misgivings. At times he felt as if his life was complicated and tangled and he wasn't sure how to find the ends and make them whole. He often felt much of his uncertainty hearkened to the past, but what good would going back do? He had already told Hailey about Lydia. Austin's death was far in the past and had no bearing on his and Hailey's relationship.

"Now can we go get my wings my mommy gave me?" Natasha said, tugging on his hand, pulling him into the present.

Dan pushed himself to his feet and went to the bathroom to find his daughter's precious wings.

Interesting that Natasha had no trouble melding her past and present—Lydia and Hailey. As he pulled the glittery wings out of the laundry basket he wished it were as easy for him.

When they got back, Hailey held her phone, frowning at it as if it had just given her bad news.

"Is everything okay?" Dan asked, hurrying to her side. "Is it your grandmother?"

Hailey shook her head, looking up at him. "No. It was the school that offered me that fall job. They want me to come earlier."

She looked as if she expected something from him, but he wasn't sure what to say. Did he dare encourage her to reconsider taking the job?

Were they even at that point?

Your daughter saw you kissing Hailey. You know you care about her and she cares for you.

Once again it was as if they stood across from each other with a space between them that he had to figure out how to cross.

"Can we go?" Natasha called out, rescuing them both from the uncertainty of the moment.

"Yeah. Sure," Dan said, turning to her. He bent down and kissed her on the cheek. "You be careful and listen to Miss Deacon, okay?"

"I will," she assured him. She gave him a quick hug, then with a rustle of snow pants and jacket, walked over to Hailey, tugging on her hand. "Let's go," she said.

Without another look at Dan, Hailey pocketed her phone, grabbed the knapsack and headed toward the door.

"You forgot to say goodbye to my daddy," Natasha said. "You can kiss him too if you want."

Dan groaned inwardly, but Hailey didn't seem flustered by his daughter's comment.

"See you later, Dan," she said, her smile flickering at the corner of her mouth.

"Have fun, you two," was all he said.

And as the door closed behind them, he realized they hadn't finalized their plans for tonight.

With a swish of her skis and a spray of snow, Natasha came to a halt in front of Hailey, executing a picture-perfect parallel stop.

"That was excellent," Hailey said, clapping her hands. "Very good."

Natasha beamed up at Hailey. "I'm a really good skier."

"You are."

"When can I use a snowboard like you do?" she asked, pointing her skis downhill for her next turn, arms up, knees bent, showing perfect form.

"When you know everything there is to know about skiing," Hailey said, following Natasha, the sun sparkling off the snow on the hill. "That's how I started."

They had moved from the learning hill to the bunny hill. Natasha had easily mastered the T-bar and was quickly gaining confidence going down the longer hill.

"But I know a lot," Natasha said, flashing Hailey a grin over her shoulder. "And I bet I can go on the big hill."

"I don't know about that," Hailey said. Though she was sure Natasha could easily navigate the most basic green run, she was hesitant to follow through.

Especially with Dan's warnings to be careful ringing in her ears.

"Deanna went on the big hill," Natasha announced as they quickly came to the bottom of the bunny hill. "I saw her going up with her mom and dad. And she doesn't ski as good as me."

Trouble was, that wasn't an idle boast. Natasha had more control and could stop much more quickly than Deanna could, but Deanna was with her parents, who were responsible for her.

Natasha was with Hailey, who was no relative.

But you kissed her father.

Though Hailey suppressed that thought, embarrassment still heated her face.

"I know, but I promised your dad I would take care of you."

"Natasha. Natasha."

A little girl's voice rang out and Hailey turned to see a lime green dynamo come barreling toward them. Deanna.

She snowplowed to a stop in front of them, her hands flailing as she tried to catch her balance. She grinned at them, pushing her helmet back on her head. "That was fun," she announced, then turned to Natasha. "Are you going on the chairlift too?"

Natasha made a face of disgust. "No. I'm 'posed to stay on the bunny hill."

"You can come with me," Deanna announced, turning and skating with her skis toward the chairlift.

"Hey, hold up, Deanna," Hailey called out. "Where's your mom and dad?"

"They were with my brother. They know I'm here. I told them on the radio." Deanna held up her handheld radio to show Hailey, then shoved it back into her pocket and got in the lift line.

"Honey, you can't go on the lift by yourself," Hailey said, trying to stop her. "Come back here."

"I been already. I know how to ski." Deanna got in line, working her way to the front.

Deanna was not competent enough to go on the hill by herself and Hailey doubted the liftees would stop her. Hailey couldn't believe her parents let her get ahead of them like that. She looked from Natasha to Deanna and made a sudden decision.

"Deanna, wait," Hailey called out. "We'll go with you."

"Yay," Natasha yelled, already heading toward the lift.

Thankfully, Deanna stepped out of the line and let Hailey and Natasha catch up to her. Deanna was even more headstrong than Natasha. If Hailey went along, hopefully she could control Deanna and prevent potential injury.

As they moved to the head of the line, Hailey laid down the law with Natasha's friend. "Deanna, you have to listen to me. If you don't, I'll take away your lift ticket and you won't be able to ski anymore," she warned, using her sternest voice.

Deanna glowered at her, but thankfully, from previous run-ins with Hailey in the classroom, she knew Hailey meant business and would follow through.

"Okay," she said.

When they got to the front of the line Hailey maneuvered the girls, pulling them along with her hands, and got them in place. The cables of the lift creaked, the wheels hummed, then the chair came around. Thankfully the liftee slowed the approach of the chair even more and helped Deanna on while Hailey tended to Natasha.

Then, with a whoosh, the chair swung away and off the ground. Hailey settled the girls in and lowered the metal bar with a clunk. Okay. This was it. They were committed now.

"I'd like you to call your parents on your radio," Hailey said to Deanna, once they were underway. "Tell them where we are."

Deanna nodded, pulled the radio out of her pocket and

pushed the call button. "I'm on the Crow's Nest chairlift with Miss Deacon," she said into the radio. She released the button and a female voice squawked back. "Okay, honey. Make sure you're back at the chalet at three."

And that, it seemed, was that.

"Look behind us," Deanna said as she shoved the radio back in her pocket. "We can see Hartley Creek."

Natasha looked around and gasped. "Look how high we are, Hailey." Below them lay the town, the buildings small squares along the grid of the streets, the river bisecting the town in a snow-covered ribbon of white.

"I can see my daddy's store." Natasha pointed, her movements making the chair swing.

She turned to Hailey, a huge grin on her face. "Thanks for taking me up here. I'm so excited."

Hailey smiled back and though she was glad Natasha didn't seem frightened, she sent up a prayer for safety for all of the girls.

They hung suspended in space; the only sound was the creak and hum of the motors pulling the chairs along. As their chair headed toward the top of the hill, the usual sense of anticipation gripped Hailey.

As long as she could remember she'd spent every winter weekend on this hill, either boarding or helping with the lifts to pay for her boarding. It was like her second home and it was where she and Dan had first declared they were a couple.

Her heart shifted at the thought of him and she wondered if he would ever come on the hill again. He used to have the same passion she did, the same sense of adventure. She couldn't imagine living in town and not ever going on the hill.

She wondered if he would ever get over Austin's death and, once again, wondered why it had put so much distance between them. But he never mentioned Austin's name and never talked about his brother, and she guessed that part of Dan's reluctance to let Natasha on the hill was rooted in Austin's death. Yes, Austin was his brother, but surely he would have gotten through the worst part of his grief after seven years?

When they got to the top of the hill, the dismount went smoothly and Hailey took a moment to set the girls straight as she strapped her other foot into her binding.

"Okay, girls. You have to listen to me, right?" Hailey said, putting on her sternest voice. "We are taking the easiest run, but you have to make sure you go all the way back and forth across the hill so you don't end up going too fast."

Natasha nodded and Deanna just shrugged.

"Remember what I said about your ticket?" Hailey warned Deanna.

"Yeah. I'll listen."

"Good. Now, this isn't hard, Natasha. It's like the bunny hill, only longer, so you have to stop once in a while for a rest. I'll go first and you follow me and do exactly what I say, okay?"

They both nodded and with another prayer to settle her own concerns, Hailey headed out. She looked back and first Natasha and then Deanna followed her.

After the fifth turn, Hailey allowed herself to relax. Both girls listened and did what she told them and took their time going down the large hill. By the time they got to the bottom Natasha was so excited she wanted to go immediately again.

So they did.

Natasha was in her glory and as they started down the hill for the third time she was laughing and relaxed. Another skier is born, Hailey thought, watching as Natasha made her turns a little sharper, angled herself down the hill, gaining speed.

But, thankfully, she always listened to Hailey.

Halfway down the run Hailey stopped at the edge to wait for Natasha and Deanna and to check her helmet. As she unbuckled it, she turned, and looked up.

Natasha was halfway across the open space when Deanna, who was about two turns behind, made a sharp turn and came flying down the hill. She was a blur of neon-green.

And she was out of control.

One foot lifted off the ground as she tried to make a turn to slow down. But she was moving too fast. She tried again, arms flailing. She avoided hitting a mother with her little boy, avoided an older man, but kept coming.

"Turn, turn," Hailey called out, unable to do anything else. The little girl was uphill from her. All Hailey could do was yell instructions and hope Deanna didn't plow into anyone as she tried to slow down. "Snowplow, push on your downhill edge, push, push."

Deanna tried to regain control and managed to form a snowplow. She wouldn't make it, Hailey thought, watching in horror as Deanna headed straight toward Hailey and the trees behind her.

No time to kick off her board. All Hailey could do was try to position herself to slow the girl down.

Deanna came right at her, Hailey reached out and scooped her arm around Deanna's waist. The momentum of the little girl's speed pulled Hailey off balance. They landed together, rolling down the hill, a collision of arms and legs and skis. Snow showered over them, covering Hailey's face, blinding her as she hung on to Deanna.

Hailey heard Deanna screaming as she tried to get her board under her to dig in the snow. Finally, after what seemed like an age, they skidded to a halt. In the melee Hailey had lost her helmet. Melting snow covered her face and slid down the back of her neck and pushed up the front of her jacket.

Deanna lay against her, sobbing, one ski off her foot, the other still attached.

"Are you okay, honey?" Hailey asked, hurriedly brushing the snow off her face, blinking it out of her eyes, trying to look at Deanna.

"I'm scared," Deanna wailed.

Then Hailey cranked her head around.

Natasha. Where was Natasha? Hailey yelled her name, her head whipping around as she tried to find the little girl.

"I'm here." Natasha's voice was a tiny, wobbly sound from just above Hailey.

Hailey craned her neck. Relief sluiced through her when she saw Natasha sitting on the snow a couple of feet behind her.

"Hailey. Your face," Natasha called out, pointing. "You've got blood on your face."

Hailey reached up and touched her face with her gloved hand. But she couldn't feel anything.

"Are you all okay?" A woman's voice called out as a skier came to a stop beside them. When Hailey looked up, the woman's eyes grew wide and with a few quick flicks of her ski poles, she was out of the bindings of her skis.

And as Hailey blinked again, she realized that it wasn't melting snow running down her face. It was blood.

"So you haven't seen them all afternoon?" Dan asked one of the liftees working on the small chairlift situated beside the bunny hill.

"No, man. Sorry." The kid whipped his head back, tossing his shoulder-length hair back from his face, his multipierced ears glinting in the sun. He caught the chair coming around the turn, held it and helped a couple of giggling young girls onto it. "I saw them for most of the morning. Next thing I know she booked it for the Crow's Nest."

The main chairlift going up the hill.

Dan pushed down his panic as he walked back to the chalet. Hailey knows what she's doing, he told himself. It would be fine.

Standing by the stairs leading to the chalet, a middle-aged couple waited for him. The woman wore a thin wool blazer over a skirt and leather boots and despite the sun pouring down on the mountain, she shivered, the silk scarf around her throat offering her scant protection from the cold.

The man had his hands pushed deep into his wool topcoat, his groomed and graying hair glinting in the sun.

Mr. and Mrs. Anderson. Lydia's parents. Natasha's grandparents. They had showed up at the store twenty minutes ago, demanding to see Natasha. Immediately.

Dan had explained that Hailey would bring her back when the hill was closed, but they couldn't wait to see their granddaughter and make sure she was okay.

Thankfully, his parents were able to take care of the store. So he'd led the Andersons here. And then started looking for Hailey and Natasha.

"Did you find them?" Carla asked as he walked across the snow-packed ground toward them. "We checked the rental shop, but they hadn't returned the equipment and they weren't anywhere in the main lodge or the coffee shop or the restaurant."

"It's a big place. We could easily have missed them," Dan said, squinting against the sun glinting off the snow as he looked up the main hill.

The run coming directly toward them was the easiest on

the mountain. If they weren't on the bunny hill the chances were good they were on that one.

He would have a few words to share with Hailey if that were the case. Though he hadn't specifically said that Natasha couldn't go down the big hill, it had been assumed.

Skiers and snowboarders in brightly colored coats and pants flowed down the hill, all coming from various runs, funneling toward the main chairlift. But Dan couldn't spot Natasha's bright red suit or Hailey's distinctive red-and-orange coat.

He looked over toward the bunny hill again, checking all the bodies going up and coming down but there was no one he recognized.

"What's going on over there?" Mr. Anderson asked, pointing one gloved hand toward the main run.

Dan turned and his heart flopped in his chest.

A little girl wearing a neon-green coat and pants was being led by a woman on skis. And behind her came Natasha and Hailey. Hailey had lost her helmet and she was holding something against her forehead.

Was she hurt?

"Wait here," he told the Andersons, and with his blood rushing in his ears he ran across the hill, kicking up lumps of snow as he went.

"What happened? What's going on?" he called out as he came near the little group.

"Daddy. Daddy. Hailey had an accident. Deanna ran over her," Natasha called out. "She's bleeding."

Something deep in his gut downshifted, like a truck hitting black ice. Dan's eyes flew back to Hailey holding a bloody cloth to her forehead.

"I'm okay," she called out, obviously picking up on his panic. "I'm fine."

She turned to the woman holding Deanna's hand. "Could you make sure she connects with her parents?"

The woman frowned. "You should get that cut looked at."

"It's not a big deal," Hailey assured her. "It's already stopped bleeding. Please, just get Deanna to her mom."

The woman glanced at Dan, obviously assuming he was taking over, then she nodded and she and Deanna skied farther down the hill toward the lodge.

"What happened? Is Natasha okay?" Dan hardly knew what to ask first, his heart still thudding in his chest. "Where's your helmet?"

"Natasha is fine. Deanna went out of control and I caught her and we tumbled a bit." Hailey gave him a quick grin that, he guessed, was supposed to reassure him.

But his emotions had gone through a horrible turmoil and he couldn't focus on any one feeling. As he looked down, his thoughts jolted backward and ice slid through his veins.

He and Hailey had been in he same place when the ski patrol had come off the mountain carrying Austin's body.

Now Hailey, the woman he had put in charge of his daughter, stood in front of him, blood dripping down her face as all the worst scenarios ran through his mind. So close. So close.

His emotions exploded.

Chapter Fourteen

"Natasha, Grandma and Grandpa Anderson are waiting. Take your skis off, go to them and wait for me with them," Dan said.

Hailey heard the chill in Dan's voice and an answering shiver grabbed her neck.

Natasha seemed to sense her father's anger and without so much as a whimper or pout, bent over, popped her skis off and walked down the hill where an older, very well-dressed couple stood. Lydia's parents, Hailey presumed.

Then Dan turned to her, his hazel eyes cold, deep lines bracketing his mouth.

"What were you thinking, taking her down that hill?" he snapped.

Hailey's own misgivings crowded in her mind at the anger in Dan's voice. "She did really well. And she wanted to go. She's a capable skier."

"I thought I told you to keep her on the bunny hill?" Dan kept his voice down but the ice in his gaze and the fierceness of his voice buffeted her like a blizzard.

"She's going to ski the main hill sooner or later, Dan. And I was with her the whole time." She reached out to him, touching his coat sleeve with her hand, trying to bridge the gulf that seemed to yawn between them. "She's a good skier, Dan. And nothing happened to her."

Dan looked down at her hand and Hailey saw the blood streaked on it. She pulled her hand back, curling her fingers against her palm.

Dan swallowed but didn't meet her eyes. "This place is too… It's… She's not coming here again."

Hailey heard the finality in his words, but then her own anger kicked in.

"Really, Dan? You would keep her from the most popular thing to do in this town? Where her friends will be every weekend? Don't you remember how much fun we used to have here?"

"Used to," he said, chopping the air with his hand, as if slashing past away from present.

Hailey glanced down at the bloody cloth now twisted around her hand. The cut on her forehead still stung, but the cold air probably kept it from feeling worse.

"You're upset about me and Natasha because of what happened to Austin, aren't you?" she asked, trying to understand the relentless current of his anger. When she looked up at him again she almost fell back at the cold fury stamped on his face.

"That's in the past. It's done. We're not talking about that."

As she held his flinty gaze, realization moved like a slow storm through her. Shannon's warnings about Dan's lack of communication after Austin's death flickered and gained strength. "And that's the trouble, isn't it? We've never talked about Austin."

"What's to talk about? It's basic. He got lost. He died." His gaze cut away from hers as he shoved his hands in the pockets of his coat.

But he looked away as he spoke and his voice caught on his last word.

Hailey felt as if she was within inches of grasping something that had eluded her for seven years. "I don't know if it's that simple," she said. Then she moved closer, fear skittering through her abdomen. It was as if she and Dan were staring across an abyss.

No way that was happening. Not again.

Her sister's warnings about Dan rang once again through her head, along with every other concern that wove in and out of their relationship.

"Dan, I know something important is happening between us. I don't want to lose that. I'm happier now than I've been in a long time. I don't think I'm imagining what you are feeling either."

"You're not," was his reply, and in his eyes all traces of anger had been replaced by a broken, longing gaze. "I lost too much when I lost you."

"And I don't want to lose you again," she pleaded. "But I feel like I am. And I think it has everything to do with what happened in the past. What happened with Austin."

They were surrounded by the sounds of happy laughter and shrieks of pleasure backed by the steady hum and thump of the ski lift picking up skiers and boarders. But it was as if they were captured in their own moment in time.

How could she get through to him? She felt on the verge of discovering the one thing still standing between them.

"When Austin died, I lost so much as well." Her voice broke as she reached out to him.

Dan looked at her and in his eyes she only saw emptiness and sorrow. "And that's part of the problem," he said as he took a step back and away from her.

She fought down her panic, sensing his physical movement was an echo of his emotional withdrawal. *Not again, please, Lord, not again.*

But how could she get through to him?

"Dan. We would like to go," Mrs. Anderson called out.

Dan shot a look over his shoulder, then looked back at Hailey. "I gotta go," he muttered, but Hailey didn't release him right away. Surely whatever Mrs. Anderson wanted could wait a moment?

"Please don't walk away from me," she pleaded.

His mouth set in grim lines, Dan glanced from her to the Andersons, who were now walking toward the lodge.

"Don't throw those ambiguous statements at me and then walk away," she said, pressing on. "I'm not letting you leave me again. I need you to tell me about Austin before you leave."

Dan shot her another anguished look, but then, without another word he turned and strode away, each step he took away from her falling like a hammer on her heart.

Dan stared at his cell phone for what seemed like the hundredth time. Should he try to call her?

What could he possibly say to her when his fear at seeing the blood dripping down her face had been like a blinding storm? In that moment so many things had come together. He knew how much he cared for her. He knew how much she had also lost when Austin died.

And he knew how little he deserved to hold Hailey's heart.

But he hadn't had time to sort it all out. Not with the Andersons and their threats to take Natasha hovering behind him.

After leaving the hill, they had all driven to Cranbrook, an hour and a half's drive from Hartley Creek. The Andersons had flown there from Vancouver and had rented a hotel suite there.

Dan wasn't letting Natasha go with them on her own, so he had come along. Now it was late evening and Carla and Alfred Anderson were tucking Natasha in for the night.

Dan dropped his head against the chair in the hotel suite, staring sightlessly up at the ceiling. His head ached and his thoughts were a tangle of worries and fears. His concern over the Andersons' unexpected visit battled his struggle with Hailey's anguished gaze as he walked away.

You should have told her.

And how could he in the few minutes he had? And even worse, what would she think?

If she cares for you it doesn't matter.

Dan wished it were that easy. As she had said, when Austin died, she had lost something too. As had his parents.

As had he.

Too much sorrow, he thought, dragging his hands over his face. Too much pain and grief on his conscience.

The door of his and Natasha's bedroom clicked shut and Alfred Anderson came out, his smile relaxing his features. "She's quite the girl," he said as he folded his suit jacket in half and laid it carefully over the chair. "Pretty precious to us."

Dan tried not to see that as a veiled threat and instead decided to take it at face value. "I know. She's very precious to me too."

Alfred sat down in a chair across from Dan, then sighed heavily. "I know we should have warned you we were coming, but Carla and I got scared."

"About what?" Dan said, a knot forming in his gut.

"You know what Natasha means to us," Alfred said, leaning back, looking every inch the successful businessman he was. Dan tried to keep his cool and not feel intimidated by a man wearing a suit worth more than his truck. "We need her in our life. We can't function without her."

Dan felt as if Alfred's words sucked the center out of his world. But he waited to let Alfred play his hand before reacting.

"We know you love her so I'm hoping you understand that we love her as well," Alfred continued. "And we miss her." Alfred's voice broke on that last word.

Dan felt a flicker of surprise at the unexpected emotion Alfred let slip past his businessman's facade. But as he watched Alfred lean forward and drag his hand over his face, Hailey's words slipped back into his mind. Her comments about her grandmother's relationship with her and how important that was.

"I'm sorry about that," Dan said. "But I needed to give Natasha a chance to settle in to her new life." Dan put extra emphasis on the last phrase, as if to underline the fact that Natasha's life was in Hartley Creek.

Then Alfred looked over at him and Dan saw the anguish in his eyes.

Please, Lord, Dan prayed, *let Hailey be right about the Andersons and let me and my worries be wrong.*

"I know that Carla has been pushing to get Natasha back with us," Alfred continued. "But you have to understand that my wife is a very frightened woman." Alfred pushed his hand through his hair, rearranging its neat waves. "Lydia never gave us much time with Natasha—"

"She didn't give me much either," Dan put in, leaning forward as if tensing for battle.

"I know. I gathered as much. But you have to understand she is our only granddaughter."

"But she's my daughter and I think that would hold more clout in court."

Alfred pulled back, looking surprised. "Of course it does. We don't want to take her away from you."

"That's not what I understood from Carla."

Alfred got to his feet, his expression pleading. "When you first took Natasha away, we thought we would never see her again. Carla got desperate and overreacted and I apologize for that. She would apologize as well, but she's too proud. We know Natasha is your daughter and we know you love her. All we want is some time with her. A visit now and again."

"So you don't want custody of her."

"No. Never."

That wasn't how Dan had read the situation, but Alfred's sincerity kindled the tiniest spark of hope in his heart.

"When you say now and again, what were you thinking of?" Dan asked.

"A couple of weeks in the summer. Maybe part of the Christmas break or Easter break. We'd like to come down a couple of times a year." Alfred held his hands up in a gesture of surrender. "We're open to whatever you want to give us. We have so much love to give her. Please, just give us something."

As Alfred pleaded, Dan's shoulders lowered, the tension easing out of his neck. Hailey was right, Dan thought. And she was also right in saying Natasha could not have too much love in her life. It was obvious the Andersons cared for Natasha with the same intensity his own parents did. "I think we can come to some type of agreement," he said.

Alfred blew out a sigh. "Thank you for that, Dan. That's all we want. That's all we ever wanted."

Then the bedroom door opened again and Carla walked into the room, smoothing down the wrinkles in her shirt. "She's full of stories, that girl," Carla said as she settled into a chair. Her lips tightened as she looked at her husband, then at Dan. "I missed her. I missed her more than you can know."

"Dan and I discussed this already," Alfred said. "We'll be able to see her from time to time."

Carla gave a tight nod then leaned back in the chair, one manicured hand slipping over her face. Then she turned to Dan. "I had quite the chat with Natasha. She talks a lot about this Hailey girl." Carla tilted her head to one side in question.

"Hailey. Is she the girl who was injured at the ski hill?" Alfred added.

Dan nodded, trying not to think about the terror that had clawed at him when he had seen the blood on Hailey's face. How that same terror made him blow up at her. He knew he had overreacted but who could blame him after what had happened all those years ago?

He pushed those thoughts aside. He had been struggling to move on for the past seven years. The past was over. He had enough to deal with in the present.

"Hailey is Natasha's tutor," Dan said, "And yes, Natasha is quite fond of her."

"And you?" Alfred asked.

His question dove into Dan's heart. He was more than fond of Hailey, but how could he say this to Lydia's parents?

And were he and Hailey still "dating"? After leaving her with her questions ringing in his ears? With his own pain coming back to haunt him?

"I don't know if I should be talking about Hailey to the parents of my ex-wife."

Alfred glanced at Carla, who lifted her shoulder in a light shrug, as if telling him to go ahead.

Alfred cleared his throat, then leaned forward. "We want to talk to you about that."

Guilt clutched at Dan again. "I know how our relationship started wasn't ideal—"

"That's not what we want to talk to you about," Alfred interrupted. "Lydia was the kind of girl who always went her own way, did whatever she wanted. I'm fairly sure whatever happened between you two wasn't one-sided."

Dan could only stare, dumbfounded, even more confused. "What are you trying to say?"

Alfred folded his hands over his chest, his intertwined fingers tapping on his silk tie. "We know how difficult things must have been with you and Lydia. She was our daughter and we loved her but—" Alfred's voice broke and he glanced toward Carla as if asking her to help him out.

Carla then leaned forward, her hands resting on her knees. "Since Lydia was a child, she followed her own path. Did her own thing and many of the things she did were either to spite us or to show us she didn't care what we thought. I spent hours worrying about her—where she would end up and whom she would end up with. When she met you, well, we thought her life had taken a turn for the better. We thought she had finally come to a good place." Carla cleared her throat, lifting one hand and letting it fall. "While we weren't thrilled about how your situation began, we realized that mistakes get made." Her words were meant to reassure, but they also drew up Dan's old guilt over his and Lydia's lapse in judgment.

"I'm so sorry about that," he said.

Carla waved off his apology. "Goodness knows I'm not in any position to stand in judgment of you. I know my own behavior through all of this has not been stellar. But all of that faded away when we saw what a calming influence you were in her life. We were so thankful you married her."

Dan felt as if the center of his world shifted on its axis. He had felt nothing but shame about his marriage and the subsequent breakdown, and now his in-laws were telling him how happy they were he married Lydia?

Carla then twined her fingers around each other, lowering her head, and shot him a pleading glance. "When you got divorced, we lost something precious and we also lost some of the hopes we had for Lydia. We had hoped you two would get together again, but over time we knew that wasn't happening. However, we thought you believed what Lydia might have said about us. She disliked us so much and fought with us so much we thought she would have influenced your opinion of us as well. So when Lydia died, we thought you would take Natasha away from us permanently. That's why I said… Made the threats I did."

Dan heard the fear and sorrow in her voice and, as his gaze held hers, he saw the glint of tears.

Hailey was right, he thought again.

His heart stumbled over the thought of her. She was right about Carla and Alfred.

And maybe she was right about a few other things.

He pulled his attention back to what Alfred was now saying, fighting his own desire to call Hailey.

"We do want you to know we are so thankful for the bit of stability you brought to Lydia's life." Alfred leaned forward, pleating his tie. "Though we didn't see a lot of our daughter, we were fully aware of how hard you tried to make the relationship work. You were probably the best thing that ever happened to her. And we also saw what a wonderful father you were to Natasha. How hard you worked to take care of her." Alfred shot a quick glance toward Carla. "And again, I'm sorry for the antagonistic attitude we showed you. Please understand how desperately afraid we were that we would never see Natasha again. We overreacted and we know that now."

"I would never take her away," Dan said, still trying to absorb what Carla and Alfred had told him about Lydia. What they had given him with their encouraging words. Did they really think he was the best thing that happened to their daughter? "But I was afraid too. I didn't want to lose Natasha. Because she's one of the biggest blessings in my life."

Because his other blessing was Hailey.

The thought of her sent a shaft of pain plunging deep in his soul. He wanted to call her. He didn't dare call her.

"I'm glad we could clear this up," Carla said, resting her hands on her knees, leaning toward him. "I know we put you through a lot and I don't blame you if you can't forgive us, but I'd like to ask anyway."

Dan pushed his own worries aside as he held her earnest gaze. Felt her pain.

And the anger and fear he had felt around the Andersons faded away in the face of her sorrow.

"As a Christian I know I've been given forgiveness for so much more. How could I not forgive you?"

Carla sat back in her chair, her smile bemused. "Lydia said that about you. That you were a man of faith."

"Not as much as I know I should be," Dan said, feeling a flush of regret for the times he held God at arm's length. "And I feel like I'm kind of stumbling along. But I know where my hope is and I know that, as I said, I've been forgiven for my own sins."

"Well, I know we haven't made things easy for you," Carla said. "So I thank you for your forgiveness."

Dan held her gaze, surprised at the release he felt at her words. The release of the burden of his anger. He couldn't help but feel amazed at how things had changed in the past few minutes. How the atmosphere had shifted from antagonistic to understanding.

But what was more surprising was how easy granting forgiveness became when the truth surfaced. When the Andersons had admitted some of their own wrongdoings.

As those last words settled in his mind he felt a jolt of shock. He hadn't struggled with forgiving the Andersons when they had asked. Not when he saw their own struggle with the consequences of their decisions. Forgiveness had been easy to allow when the truth was on the table.

Could Hailey feel the same if he told her everything?

Could his parents?

Dan shot a glance at the clock and got up from his chair. "Please excuse me, I'd like to go tuck my daughter in." And then he had a few phone calls to make.

As Dan walked toward Natasha's room, his step felt lighter, his heart less heavy. He thought of Hailey and he sent up a prayer.

Show me what to do, Lord. Please give me a chance to fix things between us.

He waited a moment, hoping for some miraculous answer or maybe even to hear his phone ring, with Hailey on the other end, laughing and telling him she forgave him for leaving her behind at the ski hill.

But nothing.

Natasha lay in bed, beaming at him. "I'm so happy to see Gramma and Grandpa Anderson," she said, weaving her fingers together. "I missed them."

"And they missed you, punkin," Dan said, sitting on the edge of the bed, relief easing the stress in his shoulders. This part of his life, at least, was working the way it should. The Andersons weren't his enemy. Not anymore.

"Can you sing me our song?"

Our song. The one Hailey meant for our children. Dan faced a surge of fear and desolation. What if she never wanted to talk to him again? What if she was going to take that job and leave immediately?

He pushed his questions aside. He couldn't deal with them right now. He had asked God to show him what to do. For now, he had to leave the rest in God's hands.

Dan sat down beside his daughter, pulling her close. He drew in a slow breath, then sang the song, surrounded by memories of earlier times. More innocent times.

As he sang, Natasha's eyelids grew heavy, sleep finally claiming her. He held her a moment longer, inhaling the little-girl smell of her freshly washed hair, the brand new flannel nightgown Carla had brought along for her.

But as he laid his little girl down onto the bed Alfred and Carla's words resonated through his head.

You were the best thing that had happened to Lydia.

Could that really be? Could the relationship that was ignited and instigated by his guilt over Austin really have become a blessing? Could an association that had rung the death knell on Hailey's love for him—could God have used it for good?

He pinched the bridge of his nose, trying to reorient himself. For so long he had seen his relationship with Lydia as a failure, and it had become a reason to stay away from Hailey.

But he'd had it wrong. He'd taken on something he shouldn't have. He'd let false guilt stand in the way of his love for Hailey and in the meantime he'd hurt her and betrayed her again.

"Don't walk away from me." Her words echoed in his mind. Though he knew he had to go with the Andersons at that moment, at the same time he had left her. Had left her with questions he knew he didn't dare answer.

He covered his face with his hands, turning to the one source of strength and forgiveness that had always been in his life.

Please, Lord, he prayed, *I've prayed for forgiveness for Austin before. I'm asking for it again. Help me to feel it. Let me find a way to talk to Hailey. To explain. Let me find a way to let go of the guilt between us. And help her to understand.*

Chapter Fifteen

Hailey dropped her knapsack on the floor and rolled her neck, easing the kink out of it. The first day of the school week had been long and tiring.

And depressing.

All morning she'd felt as if she was waiting. Every slam of the classroom door, every glimpse of a man's figure, set her heart into high gear. But neither Dan nor Natasha had shown up and Hailey had resolutely forced herself not to go digging through her knapsack to find her cell phone to call him.

She walked to the frosted window of her living room, pressing her heated forehead to the chilly glass. From here, if she angled her head just right, she could see the ski hill. And if she moved a foot to the right, she could catch a glimpse of the top lefthand corner of the brick building that housed Dan's hardware store and apartment.

She pushed herself away from the window and grabbed her knapsack. All morning she had resisted the urge to call Dan. She wasn't chasing after him. Especially when he hadn't called to talk to her either.

Was it over between them?

She wasn't sure. She just knew what she had gone

through the last time he had walked away from her and then not called. She wouldn't allow that to happen again.

With a toss of her head, she grabbed her knapsack. She was calling that lady back. Telling her she was taking the job. This time she would be the first to leave Hartley Creek.

She walked into her bedroom, dropped her knapsack on the bed and, as she did, she saw her Bible lying on the bedside table. Last night she'd been too tired and too over-wrought to read it. She reached for her knapsack to get her phone.

Don't call yet.

So what do I do instead?

Think about this. Pray about it.

Easing out a sigh she picked up her Bible and, on impulse, turned to the passage the pastor had read in church yesterday morning. Before she'd gone to get Natasha. Before everything had fallen apart.

She looked down at the Bible and started reading at verse 5 of Psalm 36. As she read, her hand clutched the necklace her Nana had given her, as if anchoring herself to the stories of the past while she dealt with the present.

> *Your love, Lord, reaches to the heavens, Your faith-fulness to the skies. Your righteousness is like the highest mountains, Your justice like the great deep. You, Lord, preserve both people and animals. How priceless is Your unfailing love, O God!*
> *People take refuge in the shadow of Your wings.*

Hailey rested her finger on the passage, reading and re-reading them. *Your righteousness is like the highest mountain.*

She lowered her head, pressing her fingers against her

eyes. "Please, Lord," she whispered. "Help me to trust in Your faithfulness and Yours alone. Help me to know that Your righteousness and Your love are more secure and strong and powerful than the tallest mountains surrounding our valley. Help me to know that Your love is more secure than any man's."

She felt a sob catch in her throat as she thought of Dan. She kept seeing him walk away from her, leaving her with echoes of Austin once again resounding between them.

Left behind again.

Those words had a nasty curl to their edges and part of her didn't want to believe it. Yes, Dan probably had a good reason for leaving and she imagined that his controversy with the Andersons had much to do with the physical distance he had put between them.

But he had left her in other ways as well. He hadn't called. He hadn't tried to connect.

But neither have you. A cord of three strands is not easily broken.

The words resounded through her mind. She had separated herself from Dan as surely as he had separated himself from her. She didn't go after him, or give him the benefit of the doubt.

Yes, her father had left her when she was a child, and yes, Dan had left her once before.

She clutched her necklace again, thinking back to her ancestor August. A man who had swallowed his own pride and made the trek back to the woman he loved. He had chosen love.

Maybe she needed to make some move herself.

With this resolve burning in her soul she took her backpack and upended it to get her phone.

This time she was not idly sitting by and letting Dan set the conditions. She was not allowing the cord they had been weaving to be torn apart again. Before she called back to take that job, she was calling Dan to give him one more chance to make things right between them.

But five minutes later, with every pocket searched and every item in her backpack sorted on her bed, she realized her phone was not here.

She got up and checked her bed. Checked the floor. Then she remembered tucking her phone in the pocket of her coat after the school had called her to see if she could come sooner. She ran to her snowboarding jacket and shoved her hands in the pockets.

Nothing.

She leaned back against the door of her apartment, still clutching her jacket. Where could her phone be? How could she have lost it?

She mentally retraced her steps from the time she'd put the phone in her pocket until she'd realized it was missing. And then realization dawned.

When Deanna had run into her on the ski hill, her phone must have fallen out of the pocket of her jacket into the snow. But what were the odds of her finding it again?

She didn't care. She had to try. She needed to know if he'd been trying to call.

She quickly changed into her snow pants, swapped her school shirt for a merino wool top, shrugged on her jacket, snagged her snowboard and headed out to the hill. Thankfully, her car was finally fixed so she had her own transportation.

The sun eased its way down toward the horizon when she got off the chairlift at the top of the run she had taken Natasha and Deanne down only yesterday. She stood there a moment, allowing the waning warmth of the sun to ease away the chill that had enveloped her soul since she'd watched Dan walk away. When she found her phone, she would know if he'd really meant to abandon her.

The hill was quieter than yesterday. Most of the week-end tourists were back in Calgary, Lethbridge, Cranbrook or wherever they had come from.

She twisted her board downhill, then let gravity do its work. The wind whistled through her hair as she carved quick turns, the snow spraying out from her board with each twist of her body.

She missed this so much, she thought. But more than anything, she missed doing this with Dan. Her heart stuttered at the thought of him.

And as she neared the spot where she was sure Deanna had run into her, she slowed down, praying she would find her phone.

Praying there would be a message on it from Dan.

She came to the area and loosened her bindings, stepping out of her board. She looked over her shoulder, trying to recreate the scene. The odds were not in her favor. How many people had gone over this spot since? But it was close to the trees and maybe. Just maybe.

She first walked a circle around the area, going into the trees, then back onto the hill. Nothing. She started kicking up the snow in the vain hope she would find something.

Nothing.

This was silly. Just go to the chalet and call him.

Maybe she needed to take a leap, here. Trust that going back to Dan was right, whether or not he'd come to his senses.

Searching for her phone was obviously futile. She knew her pride was getting in the way.

She walked over to her board, stepped in the bindings and then as she bent over to tighten them she caught a flash of metallic pink winking back at her. She pushed the snow aside and with a triumphant grin, pulled her cell phone out of the snow.

She pushed it into her shirt against her stomach to warm it up, her heart beginning a nervous pounding. What if the phone was broken? What if Dan hadn't called her? She took a deep breath. She already knew what she had to do, regardless.

When the metal no longer gave her a chill she pulled the phone out and hit a button that woke it up. The screen flickered, wavered and then shone back at her.

Twelve missed calls.

With trembling fingers she checked the call log. One of the calls was from Shannon. One from her Nana.

And ten were from Dan.

She sat down in the snow, her legs giving way, her heart fluttering in her chest. He hadn't left her. He hadn't forgotten about her.

Then the phone sent its tinny song ringing into the silence. Hailey started, her fluttering shifting into pounding.

She glanced at the call display.

Dan.

"Hello," she said, frustrated with the weakness of her voice.

"Hailey. Finally."

Did she imagine the relief in his voice?

"Where are you?" he asked.

"I'm on the hill."

Silence followed and she found herself tensing, curling her toes up in her boots, clenching a fist.

"Can you wait there for me?"

"Okay." She hated how shaky that single word sounded. She cleared her throat, got a grip and continued. "Where do you want to meet?"

"Top of Monnihan?"

"On the hill?" Dan hadn't been on the hill since Austin died.

"Yes. If that's okay."

She hardly dared think what this might mean.

"Yeah. Sure. I'll be waiting."

"I'll be there in about half an hour."

She took a quick glance at her handset. "That's cutting it close. Crow's Nest chairlift shuts in forty-five minutes."

"I'll be there. Just wait for me, please?"

She wanted to ask why, but that would waste time. So she simply said yes, and disconnected. When she put the phone in her pocket she made sure to zip the pocket shut. Then she pushed herself to her feet, trying to work her head around what was going on.

Dan was coming to the ski hill.

"We're closing the lift down." The liftee held up his hand as Dan came up to the Crow's Nest Chair.

Dan slipped on his gloves, his heart still pounding from running all the way from the ticket booth. He caught a few breaths as he watched the chairs still moving up the mountain, holding skiers. He held up his ticket and looked the kid, much younger and about a foot shorter, in the eye. "I bought this ticket five minutes ago. The girl who sold it to me said the lift would be running for another fifteen minutes."

With a rustle of his baggy snow pants, the kid shifted his weight, snapped his gum and shrugged. "Yeah, but that's only for the people on the chair already. I'm not letting anyone else on."

Dan stifled the urge to grab the kid and throttle him. Hailey was waiting and he wasn't letting her down. Not again. He looked up the hill, then slid a bit closer to the kid, smiled down at him. "I've been skiing and boarding on this hill since you were in diapers. I know this lift doesn't shut down until four and it ain't four."

The kid just stared at him.

"I'm getting on the lift."

"You can't."

"Try and stop me."

Dan pushed himself past the kid and jumped onto the first chair that came around.

"Hey, you can't do that," the kid yelled. "I told you it was closing."

Dan ignored him, knowing the kid wouldn't stop the lift, not with all the other people still on it, though he had to suppress a laugh at his own daring. For someone who routinely drove five miles an hour under the speed limit, paid his taxes even before they were due and always came to a full stop at a stop sign, this was daring indeed.

And he didn't feel the least bit sorry.

Hailey was waiting for him.

He wanted to call her, to make sure she was still there but resisted the urge. Anything he had to say to her from here on had to be said to her face.

The lift creaked and groaned as his chair headed toward the top. The muted humming of the cables pulled back memories of hours and days spent on this hill. He looked below him, watching the more adventurous and reckless kids, skiing and boarding down the packed snow below the lift. Their laughter and squeals reminded him of the adventures he and Hailey undertook.

In spite of his resolve, memories of Austin wove themselves through them.

Seven years later, memories of his brother, of that day, could still sting and accuse. He struggled to put that aside. Then he sat back in the chair and did the only thing he could while he waited. He prayed.

After what felt like hours, he finally got to the top of the hill and slid off. No sooner had he touched the ground, the lift creaked and then groaned to a halt.

Dumb kid shut it down early anyway. But Dan didn't care. He had made it.

He tightened his bindings, and looked around a moment, orienting himself.

Seven years later. As he stood on this first ridge of the mountain, it felt as if he had never been gone. The angle of the lowering sun cast waiting shadows. The day was winding down.

Below him he saw the town of Hartley Creek. His hometown. The place he had run away from all those years ago. He was back now and he was back on the hill.

In spite of the weight of what lay ahead of him, he felt euphoria build as he pushed himself off, snow swishing under his board, the cool air whistling past him. He faltered a moment as he caught an edge, regained his balance, and then he was carving down the hill, shredding snow, heading off toward Monnihan.

Where Hailey waited.

Just then Dan caught a flash of orange as a kid zipped past him on his snowboard, almost cutting Dan off. He resisted the urge to yell at the kid to be careful, then frowned as the boy headed directly toward the ropes marking off the area that was off-limits.

The boy didn't look back and without hesitation lifted the rope and ducked under.

"Hey, where are you going?" Dan called out.

The kid looked back over his shoulder. He couldn't have been more than fourteen or fifteen. Younger than Austin was.

"Come back here," Dan called. "That area is out of bounds."

The kid turned, then with a swish of his board, disappeared over the white ridge. Dan hesitated a moment, wondering what to do. He thought of Hailey, waiting for him, then thought of the kid heading into an area that he knew would be dangerous.

You haven't boarded in ages. You'll just cause more problems.

But Dan couldn't ignore the voice in his head that nagged at him. What if something happened to that kid?

Dan glanced down the hill one more time, apprehension over Hailey fighting his need to at least keep an eye on the young boy. He made his decision, then ducked under the ropes and followed the tracks through the fresh powder.

The boy was going fast. Dan had pushed himself beyond his comfort level, but was pleased to feel his old skills returning. He was never the flashy boarder Hailey was, but he always managed to stay ahead of her in powder.

He carved over, cut a quick turn to avoid some trees, then hit an almost vertical slope. His heart jumped in his throat as he made his way down, his every nerve on alert, his heart lifting in his chest.

He caught a glimpse of orange, yelled again but the boy didn't slow down. Dan pushed himself to go a little faster to keep up.

He maneuvered past a clump of trees, heavy and white with snow, cut a sharp curve and then stopped.

He couldn't see the boy anywhere. Frowning, Dan scanned the hill again, following the tracks.

Then ice flowed through his veins. The tracks led to a tree and then disappeared.

Dan pushed off, heading straight down the hill, the wind whistling past him. He struggled to maintain control, adrenaline surging through his arteries.

He got closer and his suspicions were confirmed. All he

could see sticking out from the snow around the tree was the edge of a snowboard. The boy had fallen into a tree well, a deep snow depression around the tree, and was now probably lying upside down, covered in snow. Dan stopped, took his board off and carefully approached the tree well.

"Can you hear me? Don't move," Dan called out. "Don't move at all. You'll just shake down more snow. Just lay still."

His heart plunged when he heard a muffled cry. The boy was still alive.

If he didn't pull the boy out soon he would suffocate. But if Dan wasn't careful he would end up stuck himself.

"Listen to me. Don't move," Dan repeated. "Stay calm. I'll get you out but you can't move." Dan went below the well, grabbed his board and shoveled snow away from the hole as fast as he could. "Don't move," he called out while he worked.

Dan forced himself to breathe, to make his movements steady and sure but his limbs felt like they were moving through syrup, his hands couldn't go fast enough. Thankfully, the boy's snowboard was lodged in the snow like an inverted bridge, preventing him from going farther down into the tree well. This high up the snow base was meters thick and the open area under the tree was also that deep.

Dan pulled, and when he felt a shift, he pulled harder. Finally, after what seemed like hours he managed to drag the boy free.

"Take a breath," Dan urged, rolling the boy onto his back. "Just relax and take a breath."

The boy, his face crusted with snow, coughed, sputtered, gasped and coughed again.

Dan sat back in the snow, his limbs like limp spaghetti. He had to breathe himself. Had to force himself to relax.

Thank you, Lord, he prayed as he drew in another shaky breath.

The boy coughed again, then jerked to a sitting position. "What happened?" he gasped, glancing wildly around as if getting his bearings again.

"You fell into a tree well." Dan forced himself to breathe again, his thoughts a jumbled whirl of relief, prayers and beneath all that a slow stirring of anger.

"A what?" he asked, his voice a timid sound.

Dan's anger grew. "You went boarding out of bounds and you don't know what a tree well is?"

The boy coughed again as he shook his head and Dan could see that his face had turned as pale as the snow they sat on.

"See how the branches of these spruce trees flare out?" Dan asked. "They're like an umbrella and keep the snow from gathering under the tree so there's this open space under the branches that forms a pit. This mountain gets an average snowfall of nine hundred seventy centimeters— that's thirty-one feet if you don't do metric. The snow around the tree is powdery. You get too close to the tree and you get sucked into the snow and dumped, usually upside down, in a hole deeper than you are tall. And there's a bunch of trees in these out-of-bounds areas, all of them with a well around them." Dan heard his voice rise and stopped himself.

The kid looked scared enough. He was still breathing heavily, his eyes wide and dark.

"What if you didn't follow me?" he asked, his voice wavering with fear.

Dan held his gaze a beat, as if to underline what he was about to say. "You would have died from suffocation because there's no way you could have gotten out of that well on your own."

It didn't seem possible for the boy's face to grow any whiter but it did. He blinked a couple of times, before giving in, dropping his face into gloved hands with a sob.

Dan watched him for a moment, then, taking pity on him, moved closer and put his hand on the boy's shoulder, giving him a hard squeeze.

"You're okay."

The boy dragged his gloved hands over a face streaked with tears. "Thanks. Thanks for saving my life."

The words shifted something deep within Dan as the reality of what had happened only now seemed to settle. If someone had followed Austin, would he still be alive?

"What's your name?" he asked the young boy.

"Jeremy. Jeremy LeBron," the boy said, his voice still shaking.

"Well, Jeremy, you okay to keep boarding?"

Jeremy glanced back at the tree well and the disturbed snow around it and drew in a shaking breath. "I don't know."

"You'll be okay if you follow me," Dan said, getting to his feet. He didn't want to take the chance that the ski patrol would come and find them. They had to get back to the main hill before it got too dark.

Jeremy slowly got to his feet, wavered a bit and then nodded.

"Okay. Let's get you down the hill." He glanced around to get his bearings. Near as he could tell, if they traversed the hill they could hit the mountain at the top of Monnihan run.

And hopefully Hailey would still be waiting there. He pulled out his cell phone to call her to let her know. His heart sank in his chest. No bars. No reception.

He tucked his phone back in his pocket, then pushed off across the hill, Jeremy right behind him.

Please, Lord, let Hailey still be waiting, he prayed.

Chapter Sixteen

Hailey pulled her knees close, digging her board in the hill. She'd been sitting here, at the top of Monnihan run, for twenty minutes now. Dan should have been here long ago.

She glanced at her phone again, wondering if he would call her. Wondering if she should call him.

He knows exactly where you are, she thought.

So where was he?

Hailey glanced down the hill, now empty of skiers, the chairlifts swinging lightly in the ever-present mountain wind. In a couple of minutes the ski patrol would make their last sweep of the hill, urging all the laggards down to the bottom, checking for injured skiers and boarders.

The sun was easing down toward the mountains. Soon it would be dusk.

How long should she wait? Should she wait?

He'd said he was coming.

But behind her confident declaration came a chilling thought. What if he changed his mind? And on the heels of that, what if something had happened to him?

Hailey felt a flutter deep in her stomach as she looked down the empty run below her. She could see the figures of the last skiers and snowboarders standing at the bottom of the hill, done for the day.

Please, Lord, let Dan come.

She felt as if all she'd done since Dan had called her was send up simple, formless prayers. Because she wasn't sure what to pray for.

She pulled out her phone and checked but there was nothing.

The familiar swish of a board caught her attention and her heart. She spun around and then with a spray of snow, a red-coated ski patrol stopped by her. Though he wore a helmet Hailey recognized Jess Schroder, a fellow boarder whose father owned the ski hill.

"Everything okay?" Jess called out, looking down on her.

She wanted to smile up at him and say yes. She wanted to believe that Dan wasn't here simply because he was late.

"Have you seen Dan? He's wearing a blue coat, black pants, riding a black snowboard?"

Jess leaned on his poles and pushed his goggles up on his helmet, his blue eyes squinting against the glare off the snow. "No, sorry, Hailey. Haven't, though I've got a couple of guys checking out some tracks that went out of bounds about hundred feet above here."

Hailey hugged her knees, chewing on her lip. Was that Dan? She dismissed that thought. Dan would never take a chance like that. He knew she was waiting.

"But sorry to say," Jess said to her. "The hill is closing. You've got to get to the bottom."

Hailey reluctantly got to her feet just as Jess's radio on his shoulder squawked.

"Yeah. Jess here," he said.

"Got a couple of guys here, heading toward you. Looks like one of them ended up in a tree well," the tinny voice over the radio replied. "We're following the tracks to make sure they get onto the hill okay."

Hailey wanted to grab Jess's radio and ask who it was. What did they look like? Where were they?

"I'll wait," Jess said.

"Can I wait too?"

Jess looked down on her from his considerable height, pursing his lips. "Yeah. Sure."

Hailey wanted to hug him but contented herself with a quick smile.

She turned to the trees edging the run, her heart pounding in her chest, willing, praying for someone to come out.

The air grew cooler and a few flakes began drifting down.

"Supposed to get primo powder up here tomorrow," Jess said, leaning on his poles. "Be great for the Cat skiing."

Hailey wrapped her arms around her waist, unable to make small talk with him, her entire attention focused on the trees. She didn't know where the late skiers would come out and she didn't know if one of them was Dan. All she could do was watch and send out small, unspecific prayers.

Please, Lord. Please, Lord.

And then she saw a figure burst out of the trees, duck under the rope marking the boundary, then turn and hold it up. He wore a blue coat and black pants. Hailey's heart turned over and she pushed off just as a young boy came out from the trees and ducked under the rope Dan was holding up.

"Dan. What happened?" Hailey called out, heading directly toward him, her heart dancing against her ribs, relief and happiness battling with each other.

"Jeremy here ended up in a tree well," Dan said as th young boy came to a halt beside him. His coat was cr with snow and Hailey could see the fear still etched on his features.

Jess was beside them, pulling off his pack.

"You okay?" he asked the kid, then turned to Dan. "Nothing broken?"

"Nope," Dan replied, drawing in a deep breath. "He's okay far as I can tell."

The boy shook his head and turned to Dan. "This guy saved my life. I thought I was going to die."

"You would have if you'd been on your own," Jess said, his deep voice full of reprimand. "Let's head down the hill. We'll check you over at the bottom."

Just then the other ski patrol members emerged from the trees.

"We'll all go down together," Jess said. He looked over at Dan and Hailey. "You'll have to come too."

Hailey nodded, then glanced at Dan, relief sluicing through her. He hadn't forgotten about her. He hadn't abandoned her.

They said nothing as they carved their way down the hill. They were just about at the bottom when Dan caught Hailey by the arm.

"I need to talk to Hailey," Dan said, when Jess stopped, shooting him a questioning glance. "And I want to do it up here. On the hill."

Jess glanced up and down. The chalet was within view. "Okay, but I'll be watching to make sure you make it down."

"Fair enough," Dan said.

Hailey felt a thrum of anticipation as the ski patrol took le_____ ____ther down the hill, disappearing over a ridge, _____ _____earing at the very bottom.

_____ _____pped down onto the snow and pulled Hailey __ ___e him. "Hey. So. Here we are. Full circle."

A silvery fragment of happiness, bright as the sparkling snow around them, pierced her heart.

"Hey, yourself," she returned. "Are you okay?"

"Trying to be," he said, pulling in a wavering breath. "Seeing that kid upside down in that tree well took ten years off my life." He pulled his helmet off and rubbed his eyes with his fist. Then he drew in another breath and looked over the valley below them. "In spite of that, I missed this."

Hailey's questions and thoughts tumbled over one another, all demanding to be spoken. But she kept quiet and waited for Dan.

They sat for a few more moments, as if letting the time between them catch up to this moment, this completing of a circle of events that had sundered their lives.

Then Dan reached over and ran his fingertip above the cut on her forehead, now covered with a couple of Steri-Strips. "Are you okay?"

"I'm fine. It stung a bit but Shannon said it wouldn't scar. Not that I care about that," she added, in case he might think her vain.

Dan let his finger drift down her face, then, to her disappointment, he withdrew his hand, and turned his eyes back to the valley.

Hailey let the moment lengthen, knowing that after all these years, Dan would need some time to begin. For now, she was content to be beside him, sitting on the ski hill.

"I don't know where to start," he said finally, his words quiet. "I'm not sure exactly what to say."

Hailey swallowed, then said, "Why don't you start with Austin?"

"That's probably the best place to begin." Dan waited a moment, then turned to Hailey. "Remember how we got separated on the lift that day?"

She nodded. "You and Austin ended up together with some girl and I was trying not to be jealous."

A melancholy smile tweaked his lips. "You never needed to be jealous."

Hailey returned his smile, his words like a gift.

"Anyhow, when Austin and I got to the top," Dan continued, "I told him to find some friends to go boarding with. I wanted to be alone with you. I had something important I wanted to ask you."

Hailey couldn't help it. Even after all this time, her heart beat with a sense of expectation.

"But Austin didn't want to go. He wanted to be with you." Dan looked down at his hands, shaking his head lightly. "I don't know if you ever noticed, but my little brother had a huge crush on you."

This was news to Hailey. "No. I had no idea."

"That's why he always hung out with us. I guess he was hoping, somewhere along the way, that you'd notice him or that you'd get rid of me and go with him." Dan stopped there, pressing his lips together. He blinked once, dashed his hand over his eyes and eased out a slow breath. Hailey sensed how difficult this was for Dan but also knew they were on the verge of something important and necessary to their relationship.

That last word caught in her mind, full of hope and possibilities. But she caught herself. Just wait. Just wait.

"I was mad at him because all day I'd been trying to get rid of him and he wouldn't take the hint. I had...I had a ring I wanted to give to you. A promise ring. A way of letting you know you were mine." He paused again and Hailey clung to his words, holding them close. "Anyway, Austin wasn't getting the hint and I was getting more and more frustrated with him. So while we waited for you I told him that I wanted him to leave us alone. Take a hint and take a hike and stop being so ridiculous about his feelings for you. That you would never have anything to do with him. I didn't hold back." He paused, lowering his head in his hands. "I'll never forget the look on his face when I said that. He looked as if I had punched him in the stomach. Then he pushed off and the next thing we knew, he was gone. And the last thing he heard from me were those hateful, awful words that probably caused his death."

Dan's voice broke and Hailey felt all the pain and guilt Dan had been carrying around all those years.

And suddenly it was as if the sun had come from behind the clouds, illuminating all the doubts and concerns she'd had all those years.

"So that's why you pulled away from me? Not just because you lost Austin but because you thought you caused his death?"

"I kept going over and over what I said to him, wishing, praying I could back up and do it all over again. It was like every word I said was a punch that pushed him to the edge." Dan stopped, his voice cracking. He cleared his throat and continued. "I couldn't talk about it either to my parents or you. I couldn't let you find out what kind of person I really was. The only way I could deal with what I did was to push you away too."

Hailey felt her own regret move slowly through her, picking up emotions as it gained strength. "And I broke up with you. I couldn't be bothered to understand. To understand or to wait until you got through this all. I'm sorry."

He turned to her then, taking her hand in his, covering it, his eyes holding her like a tack. "Don't apologize. You have nothing to apologize for. I told you I was leaving Hartley Creek, what else could you do?"

"I could have been more understanding...but I was scared. Scared that you were leaving me like my father did. That's why I broke up with you. Because this time I wanted to be the one to do it first."

Then Dan caught her face in his hands. "So much pain and sorrow..." He let the sentence trail off. "So much misunderstanding."

His eyes held hers, delving deeply into her soul. "I'm so sorry for everything. Would you forgive me?"

She held his broken, longing gaze and her heart leapt in her chest. "I have nothing to forgive you for and everything to love you for."

Then, to her surprise, he pulled her closer, lowered his head and caught her lips in a cool, gentle kiss. A kiss which connected them and calmed the sorrow and hurt of the last few days.

He pulled away, then pressed his now-warm lips to her cheeks, her forehead, then her mouth again.

Hailey clung to him, her soul singing with joy and wonder.

This was right, she thought. This was how things were supposed to be.

He finally pulled away. "I love you, Hailey Deacon. I love you so much. Always have." He sighed. "I've got so much more to tell you, so much more to talk about. I want to spend the rest of my life loving you. Telling you what you mean to me."

Hailey's heart skipped. Had she heard him right?

He kissed her again. "I hope I'm not jumping the gun, but I don't want this to end, ever. I want you to marry me."

Hailey closed her eyes, letting his wonderful, loving, amazing words rest in the silence. Letting them register in her heart.

Then she looked up at him, her smile threatening to split her face.

"Yes. My answer is yes."

He cupped her face, letting his fingers trace her features. "You are amazing to me, Hailey. I've learned so much from you."

"Well, that's a good thing, I guess. I am a teacher after all."

He grinned at her, then kissed her again.

"I'll have to go talk to my parents next. Tell them what really happened with Austin." He paused and Hailey heard the pain and regret in his voice.

She cupped his cheeks, turning his face to hers. "Dan, Austin made his own choices. You don't have to take that on. He didn't have to go down that run. You didn't push him down there, just like no one pushed that boy you just rescued down the hill. He had made his own choices too."

Dan pressed his lips together, as if still not sure.

"You've taken responsibility for seven years," she said, hoping, praying he understood. "You told me what happened and I wasn't shocked or angry. I know your parents won't be either. They're so happy you're back in their lives. You and Natasha. That's enough for them."

Dan shot her a grateful glance. "Part of me knows that. The Andersons asked me to forgive them for trying to take Natasha away."

"And did you?"

"Yeah. I did. And it wasn't that hard after all."

Hailey ran her fingers down his face, cupping his chin in hers, his whiskers rough against her hand. "Forgiveness is freedom and I know your parents, once they hear the truth, will not even think they have anything to forgive. I think they'll be glad to have the Dan they have always loved, completely back. Nothing can bring Austin back, but you didn't cause his death."

"I think a part of me always knew that," Dan said. "But

I couldn't forgive myself. And when that happened, I compounded that mistake with many more."

"But you're here now," Hailey said. "And I'm here. And you just saved a young boy's life. And maybe, if someone had been watching out for Austin like you were watching out for that kid, he might be alive too."

Dan looked at her again and she saw the beginnings of understanding in his eyes.

"I'm looking forward to starting over," she continued. "To taking care of you and Natasha."

Dan's grin expanded, and he caught her in a fierce hug. "You are such a blessing. I'm so thankful that God gave us another chance together."

This declaration was followed by another kiss and then another.

Hailey pulled back and looked down over the deserted hill, letting the peace of the moment wash over her.

Her heart sang and she folded her hands over Dan's. "Can we pray together? Right here?" she said.

"I'd like that."

Hailey tightened her grip on Dan's hand then lowered her head, drew in a breath to center herself and began.

"Dear Lord, thank You for this mountain that brought us great joy and sorrow. Help us to find our way through the sorrow. Thank You for Austin and the blessing his life was for all of us. We miss him, but we also know that he is now with You. Help us through our pain and sorrow and guilt. Thank You for using Dan to save that boy's life. Help us to embrace Your forgiveness and show us that always and everywhere, our lives are in Your hands."

She stopped, her own throat thickening as she thought of Austin and the sorrow and guilt Dan had been carrying all these years.

Dan squeezed her hand and then he began, his voice

quiet and subdued, but, at the same time, holding a power that resonated with Hailey.

"Thanks, Lord, for Hailey. Thanks for family and the town and community we're a part of. Forgive me, Lord, for what I told my brother. Forgive me for how I treated him." He stopped a moment, then continued. "Thanks for covering our mistakes. Thanks for feeling our pain. Thanks for Your love."

Dan stopped and Hailey whispered an *"Amen."*

Neither said anything, as if unwilling to break the holy moment.

Finally Hailey drew in a long, cleansing breath and gave Dan a smile. "That's the first time we've prayed together," she said.

"It's a good way to start what we're going to finish."

Hailey nodded, peace washing over her. Then she looked backward, up at the mountain, and she smiled.

"Okay, what's putting that look on your face?" Dan asked.

Hailey's smile grew. "According to my Nana, the ridge behind us is the one that August Beck come over when he came back to Kamiskahk."

Dan followed her gaze and a smile crept across his lips as well. "Very appropriate then, isn't it, that I proposed to you right here."

Hailey turned back to Dan. "He made the right choice when he came back."

Dan dropped a cool kiss on her forehead. "I'm glad I made the right choice too," he said. "I'm glad I came back."

"So am I." She kissed him back, then wrested her gloves out of her pocket, glancing around. "We're losing our light soon. I guess we better get going before Jess kicks us off the hill."

Dan grinned and touched the end of her nose. "Won't be the first time," he said.

"Race you to the bottom?" Hailey popped up to her feet and slapped the snow off her pants.

"I'm too rusty to do any racing," Dan groaned. "I'll be lucky to get to the bottom in one piece."

"Hey, I know a good snowboarding instructor. Could give you a few lessons," Hailey said with a wink.

"She already has," Dan said.

Then, together, they made their way down the hill. Toward Hartley Creek. Toward Natasha.

Toward home.

* * * * *

Dear Reader,

Dan was locked in the past even though, in his mind, he had moved on. He might have been able to push aside what had happened, but his guilt over his brother's death colored everything and influenced every decision he had made. It wasn't until he faced his past that he could be free from it.

I know there are times in my life that I think I can put something behind me and there are times I have to move on. But, as Hailey's sister said in this story, sometimes you have to go back before you can go ahead. Sometimes you have to go back to hurts and guilt that have kept you away from someone and separated you from them before you can have a proper relationship. And sometimes you need to ask forgiveness for those hurts. I pray, if this is the case in your life, that you can learn that forgiveness is something God gives us freely, when we acknowledge what we have done.

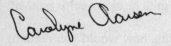

P.S. I love to hear from my readers. Send a note to caarsen@xplornet.com. Or visit my website at www.carolyneaarsen.com. Make sure to check out the latest news at the Hartley Creek Herald.

Questions for Discussion

1. Why do you think Dan was reluctant to have Hailey tutor his daughter?

2. What was your reaction to Natasha's behavior? Why do you think she acted the way she did? How would you have dealt with her?

3. Hailey and Dan had a history that went back to high school. Have you had a high school sweetheart? Why do you think high school romances stay with us so long?

4. Why do you think Hailey wanted to leave Hartley Creek when she had family there?

5. Why did Dan take on the guilt he had over his brother?

6. If you were Dan's parents, how would you react to what happened between him and Austin?

7. Why do you think Dan was so reluctant to face the past?

8. Why do you think Hailey was so reluctant to let Dan back into her life?

9. What is your opinion of the statement in the book, "Sometimes you have to go back before you can go ahead"?

10. Have you ever had to deal with guilt that you have pushed to the past? How did you handle it, or are you still burdened with it?

INSPIRATIONAL

Love Inspired

REQUEST YOUR FREE BOOKS!

2 FREE INSPIRATIONAL NOVELS
PLUS 2
FREE
MYSTERY GIFTS

Love Inspired

YES! Please send me 2 FREE Love Inspired® novels and my 2 FREE mystery gifts (gifts are worth about $10). After receiving them, if I don't wish to receive any more books, I can return the shipping statement marked "cancel." If I don't cancel, I will receive 6 brand-new novels every month and be billed just $4.49 per book in the U.S. or $4.99 per book in Canada. That's a saving of at least 22% off the cover price. It's quite a bargain! Shipping and handling is just 50¢ per book in the U.S. and 75¢ per book in Canada.* I understand that accepting the 2 free books and gifts places me under no obligation to buy anything. I can always return a shipment and cancel at any time. Even if I never buy another book, the two free books and gifts are mine to keep forever.   105/305 IDN FEGR

Name	(PLEASE PRINT)

Address	Apt. #

City	State/Prov.	Zip/Postal Code

Signature (if under 18, a parent or guardian must sign)

Mail to the **Reader Service:**
IN U.S.A.: P.O. Box 1867, Buffalo, NY 14240-1867
IN CANADA: P.O. Box 609, Fort Erie, Ontario L2A 5X3

Not valid for current subscribers to Love Inspired books.

**Are you a subscriber to Love Inspired books
and want to receive the larger-print edition?
Call 1-800-873-8635 or visit www.ReaderService.com.**

* Terms and prices subject to change without notice. Prices do not include applicable taxes. Sales tax applicable in N.Y. Canadian residents will be charged applicable taxes. Offer not valid in Quebec. This offer is limited to one order per household. All orders subject to credit approval. Credit or debit balances in a customer's account(s) may be offset by any other outstanding balance owed by or to the customer. Please allow 4 to 6 weeks for delivery. Offer available while quantities last.

Your Privacy—The Reader Service is committed to protecting your privacy. Our Privacy Policy is available online at www.ReaderService.com or upon request from the Reader Service.

We make a portion of our mailing list available to reputable third parties that offer products we believe may interest you. If you prefer that we not exchange your name with third parties, or if you wish to clarify or modify your communication preferences, please visit us at www.ReaderService.com/consumerschoice or write to us at Reader Service Preference Service, P.O. Box 9062, Buffalo, NY 14269. Include your complete name and address.